Witch Hollow

Sunshine Walkingstick, Book 4

Celia Roman

Bone Diggers Press
www.bonediggerspress.com

For you, the devoted Sunny reader.
It is because of your interest that this book exists.

10 9 8 7 6 5 4 3 2

1

January blustered into Persimmon like a grumpy old man hunkering down for the long haul.

I stepped out of a warm shower and into the bathroom's cooler air, and shivered up a storm. Lordy, I was getting plumb fragile in my old age if that's all it took to do me in.

I rushed through my morning ablutions, trying like the devil not to smile too big nor too much. Last night, Riley'd done ever thing 'cept tuck me into bed. He'd left me all warm and tingly, just like a feller orta do with his best gal, and like the ham fool I was, I fell asleep dreaming on how some day he might be laying right there beside me in my bed.

That grin burst out against my better judgment, and I let it. I was growing mighty fond of my sunshine-topped oak tree of a man, I was, and weren't put out about it a'tall.

Right as I was hopping around pulling a sock onto my right foot, a frantic series of thumps hit my front door. Well, dang it all. It weren't even seven in the morning yet. Family woulda come on in, 'cept Missy, and her knock was always polite as the Queen of England taking tea. Probably work, then, and even though my coffee can savings was full to the brim, I weren't so proud rich I could afford to turn down a good paying job.

Them thumps come again, louder this time, and I opened the bathroom door and hollered, "Hold your dang horses!"

A muffled male voice hollered back. "I'm a-holding 'em."

I grunted and yanked on t'other sock, shimmied into one of Daddy's old sweatshirts, and hoofed it to the door. Soon as I opened it, I knowed I was in for a spell of trouble. There stood Terry Whitehead with his bare fingers tucked into the pockets of worn jeans under a heavy canvas work jacket.

All the happy drained right outta me and I scowled at the scoundrel what'd planted Henry in my belly right before he abandoned me to the hand fate'd dealt me.

"You got a lotta nerve showing up on my stoop," I said, none too friendly.

Terry's shoulders hunched up around his ears, from the chill in the air or my voice, I had no ken. "I need your help, Sunny."

"You're about a decade past getting it."

I shut the door on that thin, mournful face of his and turned my back to it. Good riddance, far as I was concerned. I didn't care none what had him standing out on my front porch while Old Man Winter grumped and groaned. A man what'd abandon his own young'un didn't deserve no help of mine.

"My daughter's gone missing," he said, just loud enough for me to hear through the door. "Three days past. Just disappeared outta the yard. The police done give up on her already. Said if they didn't find her in forty-eight hours—"

I yanked open the door and glared at him. "I don't find

missing young'uns, Terry, and you dadgum well know it."

"Please, Sunny." His lower lip trembled, and for a second, I thought he was gonna cry. "She ain't but six years old. We searched ever where, just ever where, and can't find hide nor hair of her."

Sympathy shoved out some of the spitfire, softening my voice. "I wish I could help."

"You could if you wanted to." He yanked his ballcap off and resettled it over a buzz cut, and hot color tinted his cheekbones red. "Ever body knows you're the best dang tracker this side of Memphis."

Ever body 'cept me, I reckoned, since I knowed nothing of the sort.

"Never thought you was low enough to let a grudge stand in the way of helping an innocent kid," he continued.

That fired me up good. "Now you listen here, Terry Whitehead. I ain't letting no grudge keep me from doing nothing. The minute you walked out on me was the minute I let you go, you hear?"

His head hung in a miserable slump. "Sorry, Sunny. I'm just worried about my young'un, is all."

"Me, too," I snapped, then inhaled real sharp like and let the breath and mad out in one big huff of air. Here we was arguing over water long under the bridge with a heavy sky threatening snow, all the heat leaking outta my open front door, and Henry's half-sister missing to boot. "You might as well come on in and tell me about it while I put my boots on."

"Thank ye, Sunny," he said, real humble like, and that's when I knowed it was serious as serious could be. Folks could say a lot of things about Terry, good or bad, but the one word I never heard in the same breath as his name was *humble*.

I stepped back and let him in, then shut ever thing firm behind him. "Sit tight. I'll be right back."

I left without seeing if he sat and walked down the hallway into my bedroom, grabbed my boots off the closet floor, and snatched up Missy's ring. Heat seared my hand and

I nearly dropped it. I dropped the boots instead and fumbled 'til I held the ring up by its chain. The inset ruby glowed bright in the room's dimness, throwing out a tiny, warm halo as it gently twirled 'round.

Hunh. Never seen it do that before.

I slung it around my neck, careful to keep the ring outside of Daddy's sweatshirt, dug my phone out from under a pile of Riley's now-clean gym clothes, and called Missy. Soon as she said how-do, I said, "That ring of yourn is glowing something fierce."

She was silent for a long time, then finally said, real soft, "I'll be down in a minute."

A bad feeling sunk down into my gut, dragging it about knee deep. I always suspected there was more to Missy's ring than met the eye, what with the way she showed up outta the blue one day, claiming to be a lost hiker, and it being the most expensive thing on her person at the time. Far as I knowed, it never come off her neck 'til that no good hussy Belinda Arrowood stole it.

Missy told me real firm like to keep it close by, I thought to keep it safe, what with the stone being a genuine ruby and all. Now I had to wonder, though, more'n I ever wondered about Missy and that ring before. What was going on here, under the beatific surface my uncle's best gal showed the world? And why was it the ring warmed and glowed when magic or trouble was a-brewing?

I shook my head, stuffed my feet in my boots, and stomped toward the living room and my unwelcome guest. Time enough for them questions to find answers. Right now, I had a more pressing concern on my plate in the guise of a beau I'd thought to never lay eyes on again.

SOON AS I HIT the end of the hallway, I veered right toward the coffee pot. It was a basic countertop model, about as old as dirt, and had a single switch gracing its base, that being the on/off switch. No fancy timer for me, no sirree bob. I coulda replaced the dang thing with a newer up-to-date version so's I could wake up to piping hot coffee ever morning, but weren't no call to spend money for a comfort I could just as easily whip up on my own.

Now, if Riley made noises to the contrary, I'd be down at the WalMart buying a fancier rig faster'n spit, but what with it just being me, I'd as soon hang on to Old Faithful as part with hard earned cash.

Missy popped her pretty head through the door right about the time hot coffee started dripping into the waiting carafe. I leaned my butt against the kitchen counter, crossed my arms over my boobs, and arched an eyebrow at her. First time I ever seen her walk in without knocking first.

"Good morning, darling," she said as she slipped inside and shut the door behind herself. She was dressed like she always was this time of year, in one of my uncle Fame's cast-off flannel shirts and a pair of worn jeans. In the summer, she went barefoot, but as a concession to the cold, she glided around in boots or, like today, a set of Crocs over thick, woolen socks. Her sable hair was piled high on her head, curling ever which way but right, and her face was pale under the twin patches of pink Jack Frost had pinched into her cheeks.

I jacked a thumb over my shoulder. "Coffee's on the way."

Missy's violet eyes slid to my guest, waiting polite like on the couch, and widened a trifle, then they cut to me and widened a tad more. "I didn't know you had company."

I flapped my arm out, palm up, toward Terry. "Missy, this is Terry Whitehead. Terry, this is Fame's gal."

Terry stood up right quick and rubbed his palms on his stick-thin thighs. "Pleased to meet you, Miz Missy."

She glanced between us again. "Just Missy."

I could near about see questions buzzing around in her brain. Sharp as a tack, was our Missy. She knowed what Terry was to me and exactly what Fame'd do if he caught my former lover here, biding time under my roof.

But Missy weren't Fame, thank the good Lord above, and all she did was shake his hand real delicate, like a princess receiving a commoner.

I tucked my lips together tight as a clam, stifling the giggle threatening to burst free. Lordy, it tickled me pink when she done that.

Terry wiped his hands again, like as not 'cause he was scared half witless at the mere mention of Fame's name and didn't realize he was insulting poor Missy. His legs give out on him and he plopped his rear onto my sofa again. Almost as an afterthought, he dug around in his back pocket and fished out a wallet, then pulled a slip of paper out and held it up. It was a picture of him cheek to cheek with a smiling little girl.

"My daughter's missing," he said, so blunt Missy flinched.

"He wants me to hunt her down," I added, softening the blow as best I could. "Says the police have already give up on her."

Missy sat down beside Terry and patted his knee, then she took the snapshot and studied it good. "I'm sorry, dear. How long has she been gone?"

Terry burst into his spiel, spewing it out like a tea kettle's whistle. Behind me, the coffee maker's hiss and sizzle died down. I turned around and reached into the cabinet above the sink, pulled out three matching coffee mugs, none of 'em chipped, and poured us all some brew. Set 'em all on the kitchen table and took half a minute to admire the ocean colored mosaic Aunt Sadie's critter'd fixed it up with one night whilst I slept. Man, it'd done a pretty job. Maybe I shoulda kept it 'stead of letting my cousin Gentry take it in after his mama's body was found over on Cemetery Hill.

I shook my head, shuffled to the fridge in my still-unlaced boots, and retrieved a fresh pint of half-and-half. About that time, Terry's words sputtered and stopped like he run plumb out, and I said, "Coffee," and him and Missy stood up and relocated to the table.

I plopped the half-and-half down in the middle of the table, sat down in a rickety chair across from Terry, and pulled my own mug of coffee toward me, cupping it between my palms. "You reckon one has anything to do with t'other?" I asked Missy.

She slid another one of them speculative looks at me out of the corner of her eyes.

Terry paused with his cup halfway to his mouth. "What?"

"Never you mind," I said, kindly sharp.

"Sunshine." Missy's voice held the patience of the ages and not a whit of the scorpion's sting. She turned to Terry, her own cup of coffee held lightly between her elegant hands. "Where exactly do you live, Terry?"

He glanced at me, then set his cup down unsipped. "T'other side of Hiawassee, ma'am, just inside the North Carolina line."

"Near Hayesville?" she asked.

I nodded. "Lived there his whole life."

"Yes'm," Terry said. "I'm a Tarheel, born and bred. Settled down on a couple of acres next to my daddy when Sophie come along."

Not even a hint of envy twisted around in my gut. I raised my cup, blew across the top of steaming coffee, and watched Missy process what she was learning.

Her fingers tightened on her cup and she hummed softly, and a minute later she said, just as soft, "We're going to need a map."

"Yes'm," Terry agreed, then he cocked his head and looked at me, his brown eyes solemn. "You want I should get one?"

I eyed Missy. If her thoughts was traveling where I thought they was, we was gonna need more'n one map, and them maps wasn't the kind laying around in a convenience store. "I've got it. You go on home and tend to your wife. Let me get you a Styrofoam cup for your coffee."

I hustled Terry out as fast as polite'd let me, then sat right back down and speared Missy with my best no-nonsense stare. "Spill it. Why'd the ring get all hot when Terry showed up?"

Her eyes slid away from mine and landed on a point somewhere over my left shoulder. "Magic."

"What kind of magic?"

"The kind the ring recognizes." She lifted the coffee cup to her lips, sipped delicately, set it down on the table. Her skin was still pale, too pale by my reckoning, and her lips held a pinch I'd only rarely seen on her mouth. "It's not the first time it's warmed for you."

I sat back in my chair. No, it weren't, but it was the first time it'd done it when I weren't wearing it and facing some kind of danger. "What's it mean?"

"Trouble." The word fell between us, sharp and kinda ominous, like black clouds hovering over our heads under the trailer's sparkling white ceiling. "We need those maps. Police reports, too."

That give me pause. "Of little Sophie?"

"Of any missing child." She thunked her coffee cup against the table, then shoved her chair back and rose, and I coulda sworn something of them black clouds backlit her violet eyes. "Keep me updated on your progress, Sunshine. I need—"

She bent abruptly and pecked a kiss to my cheek, then whirled around and left, her exit as quiet as her entrance.

I sat there a while at my blue and green table, sipping coffee whilst the morning's goings on swirled around in my head and the ring burned hot and bright against my chest.

2

Much as I wanted to go charging off into the woods, I reckoned I needed to formulate some kinda plan. Plus, I wanted to take somebody with me whose nose was sharper'n mine ever been, and that meant waiting until after school was out and my cousin Libby come home from picking her young'uns up.

Cousin Libby being related on my daddy's side, the side with the painter blood. Let me tell you, finding out I was kin to a bunch of shape shifters was a whopper of a surprise. Having to kill my own grandma, her what'd killed my young'un for not carrying enough pure Cherokee to change, that'd been a heartbreaker, but I done it.

You get old enough, you realize there's some things you just can't get around doing, and that was one of mine.

So I killed my grandma and brought some peace to my daddy's birth clan, and I was making some peace of my own there, thanks to Libby and my grandpa.

I plucked a fresh spiral bound notebook outta the pile in my desk, kept for just this purpose, and grabbed a pen, then plopped my scrawny butt down in my chair and sipped coffee while I scribbled notes.

First on the list? Call Libby, but she weren't the only body what could help me. Sheriff Treadwell, Riley's daddy, owed me a favor for cleaning up a spot of mess for him over on Cemetery Hill last month. That I'd cleared Fame's name to boot weren't no never mind to me. The way I figured it, I caught the creature what'd killed a bunch of innocent tourists. That orta earned me enough favor with Sheriff Treadwell to get me an in with the sheriff in the next county over, especially once I mentioned them missing kids.

Second on my list was a trip to the Forest Service office. I had an in there, too, in the form of Dean Whittaker, a ranger what'd helped me track Billy Kildare's coon dog, God rest its bitty soul, and a passel of mountain lions a while back, when I first learned of my daddy's kin.

Riley could help, too, if for no other reason than his connections within the state and federal law enforcement agencies with local offices. I jotted his name down, though I'd see him later that evening for supper, more'n likely.

I caught myself grinning down at the little hearts I was doodling on the notebook paper beside his name and nearly kicked myself. Lordy, what was that boy doing to me?

I clucked my tongue and scrawled out some more notes, then drained my mug, rinsed it out, and set it in the sink. No time for dawdling. I weren't much for Terry Whitehead, but the least I could do for Henry's baby sister was put some real effort into tracking her down, even if a monster weren't involved. The weather this time of year could kill a young'un, what with the cold and random snow and icy rain. Dang them police officers' hides for giving up on her so easy.

Since the day was young, I decided to drive over to Terry's house, just to get a feel for the lay of the land. I went outside and started Daddy's IROC, letting the engine warm while I laced up my boots, dug out a jacket and the like, and poured hot coffee into a thermos.

The drive from my trailer to Terry's house weren't a hard'un a'tall. He lived west, just over the mountain range running along the border between Rabun County and Towns County. The morning was still a mite foggy when I hit the road, but when I topped the ridge east of Hightower, the sun popped out in a clear, blue sky. I turned the radio up and sang along to AC/DC as the IROC hummed down the mountain.

At last, I hit the outskirts of Hiawassee and the lake what'd been created from the Hiwassee River. Towns County's seat was a tiny mountain town, carved out of an area better suited for logging and fishing and other outdoor activities than any real industry. Residents got by on tourism and selling lake homes to them folks outta Atlanta and Florida what was fool enough to pay such ridiculous prices for a house by the water.

I turned right onto Highway 515 just past the Sherwin-Williams store, heading toward Hayesville, and shook my head. A fool and his money was soon parted. Only, if them people was fools, how'd they get enough money to buy a multi-million-dollar house in the first place?

It was a conundrum I never had found a good answer for.

Me and Daddy's IROC toodled up the road past the state line, turned onto Highway 64, then Carter Cove Road and bumped up it for a piece, and finally landed next to Terry's home.

To my surprise, it was a real house and new, or newer, not the rundown trailer I'd expected. I parked the IROC and got out, gandering real good at the green and tan one-story farmhouse the whole time. A woman stepped outta the front door right about then, her mouse brown hair swinging from a messy ponytail. She seemed somewhat familiar. I just couldn't quite place her.

Terry slammed outta the front door right behind her, and danged if he didn't look relieved. "You made it."

I nudged the IROC's door shut with my hip and nodded. "I couldn't hardly leave Henry's half-sister alone in the woods, now could I?"

"I'm so glad you're here," the woman said.

Terry placed his hand on her shoulder and said, "Sunny, this is my wife Ellie."

"Ellie Heaton," she added, and that's when I placed her. Ellie was Belinda Arrowood's niece by her much older brother, Belinda being an accident and some ten years younger'n her next oldest sibling. I'm sure I seen her and Ellie together somewhere, maybe at a wedding or a funeral. The area was small and there was a lotta overlap amongst friends and kinfolk.

I struggled to keep a frown off my face. Danged if I wanted to help Belinda out again, even if it was roundabout, but danged if I was gonna let poor little Sophie die in the winter wood neither.

It sure was uncomfortable, getting stuck between a rock and a hard place.

Finally, I stomped up the rock sidewalk to the porch and stuck my hand out to Ellie. "Sorry we couldn't meet under better circumstances."

"Me, too," she said softly as she gingerly touched her fingers to mine.

I let that pass for a handshake and stuck my hands in my back pockets, outta harm's way. "I figured I'd take me a quick look-see around, then I'm gonna call in the hounds."

Though I doubted very much Libby'd like being called that, seeing as how her other form was a cat.

Terry shook his head. "We already got dogs sniffing around. 'Bout to go out again, soon as Daddy gets here with some fresh'uns."

"Mine's a different breed," I said and let it go at that. No way was I gonna explain the painter side of my blood to near strangers. "I'm gonna grab them maps this afternoon and call in some favors, see if there's more kids missing."

Ellie nodded her head, right off. Up close her eyes was a watery blue and her face was thin and pinched, more'n likely because of her daughter going missing. "A couple more out this way over the past few months."

That sharpened me up a bit. "Same age?"

"About."

"A boy and a girl," Terry said. "One up in Warne, the other over toward Hanging Dog. We didn't even think of 'em 'til Fame's woman said something this morning."

The ring started warming up under my shirt. Real casual like, I tugged it out and stuck it between my shirt and jacket, so's to keep it from scorching my skin. "How old?"

Ellie shrugged one stooped shoulder. "School age."

That could mean anything, but I just nodded. I could find out later, assuming I could figure out how to get reports from the police over that way. Two different counties, both in North Carolina. Well, I'd figure it out, and if the police wouldn't lend a hand, I could always resort to gossip and Facebook.

Come to think on it, the police mighta posted missing kid information on their Facebook pages. That was as good a place to start as any.

I asked Terry to point out where they last seen Sophie and which directions they'd already searched, with dogs or without, and listened hard while he explained. Soon as he finished, he went back inside with Ellie, outta the crisp January air, and I started circling the house.

I didn't expect to find a lick of nothing and that's the pure plumb truth. Too many people been tromping through them woods and around the house for any evidence to remain, and my nose weren't near as sharp as Libby's, so I didn't expect to smell nothing neither.

While I was a-hunting, something curious happened,

though it took me a mite to notice it. Ever time I passed a certain angle from the house, Missy's ring warmed against my chest, so slight I almost missed it. When I did notice, I circled the house a few more times, swinging wider with each pass, and sure enough, it warmed in spots along a nearly straight line away from the house.

I stopped soon as I figured that out and stared in the direction it was pointing, mentally overlaying the direction with what I knowed of the area. Unless I was mistaken, it was pointing slightly south of west, toward Young Harris or maybe Blairsville, or maybe even farther south, if the sun could be believed. A whole lot of ground rested between Terry's house and either one of them towns, but I'd stake Daddy's knife on that being the direction Sophie'd wandered off to.

If she'd wandered off at all.

I smacked my thigh, heaved out a good sigh, and headed for the house. Least I could do was share the notions dug up by instinct and Missy's ring with Terry. It might give him something to go by when them dogs got here and they started searching again.

Me? I needed to find them maps and I needed to make some phone calls. My gut was jangling awful bad. I was pretty sure it was telling me there was more to Sophie's disappearance than what met the eye.

I DROVE straight by the turnoff for home and into Clayton. Seeing as how it weren't quite lunchtime yet, I figured there was time enough to roust the Sheriff and guilt trip him into helping out where he could. Good ol' Chip Treadwell and me got along about like oil and water, which was to say none a'tall, and that was just too dang bad. I was tired of being treated like a backwoods piece of trash by him, even if I was one, and I was sure as tootin' tired of the blood feud raging between him and my uncle.

Time to let sleeping dogs lie, you ask me.

I parked behind the courthouse and sauntered right up to the doors emblazoned with the Sheriff's logos and through 'em. This part of the courthouse used to be the jail. A few years back, the county'd set aside some money and built a real, modern jail down in Tiger, just past the public high school and the Rec Department. They'd then proceeded to house the overflow from Gainesville's jails to help offset some of the costs of running it, and after that, they'd built two more public schools right next door.

Seemed kindly crazy to put the county's entire public-school population within a mile of gang bangers and murderers and God above only knowed what else, but what did I know? I didn't run the county. I just paid for its running outta my taxes.

Sheriff Treadwell was in, and danged if he didn't come out to meet me. He hooked his hands on his hips and looked at me kindly wary like. "Sunny. What can I do for you?"

"I need to know about any missing kids going a coupla years back," I said right off. Since he was being as close to polite as he ever got with me, I reckoned I orta take advantage of it. "Henry's half-sister's gone missing over near Hiawassee. I was hoping you could ask around for me, maybe get some official reports and see what's what."

He nodded, rubbed his fingers over his square chin. "I should be able to this afternoon. Why don't I ask around and send anything I can find out with Riley when he goes out to your place tonight?"

A light bulb went off in my head and it was all I could do to wipe the grin off my face. That Riley musta lit into his daddy good. Probably Ann had, too. Bless her, she was a good sort and always kindness itself to me.

"I appreciate any help you can give," I said, and stuck my hand out and shook his real polite.

I think I mighta finally been getting the hang of this whole manners thing.

My next stop was the Forest Service office down in

Tallulah Falls. Dean weren't there when I arrived. Seems he took an early lunch and drove down to Hollywood for a hamburger, and I didn't blame him a'tall. I was getting mighty peaked myself and vowed to hit Micky D's soon as I picked up the right maps.

Which a young woman dressed in Forest Service green helped me do, to the best of both our abilities to sort out which quadrant maps I needed. I already had a couple, thanks to some work I done for young Billy Kildare a while back, but I needed more westerly ones. They wasn't expensive, and I coulda got 'em online just as easy, according to that young woman, but there weren't nothing like bending over a map and sliding your finger along contour lines to sort out the mind.

'Sides which, I didn't have internet access at home, though I weren't gonna tell her that, and I sure didn't wanna have to go to the library ever dang time I needed to search out a new area.

Finally, I gathered up the maps I needed and paid for my copies, then headed home. On the way, I swung through a drive through and picked up some burgers, and ate 'em as I drove west toward Persimmon.

Once home, I dumped the trash where it belonged and the maps on the kitchen table, and I dutifully checked completed tasks off my to-do list.

Organizing this end of my business was the handiest thing I ever done.

I spent a few minutes jotting down more thoughts, and between prepping stuff for that night's dinner, I read maps, beginning with the one showing the area around Terry's house. I'd look for a little while, mark my place with a little arrow post-it note, and peel taters. Look a while longer, mark my place, chop peppers and onions for the meatloaf. Look a while, mark my place, whip up some biscuits, and so on until it was time to toss the meatloaf together and put it in the oven.

It was late afternoon by then, well past the time Libby

shoulda been home, so I washed up good, put away the maps, and flopped onto the sofa while I dialed her number.

She answered on the first ring, and her voice was as sunny as I figured her smile was. "Howdy, cousin. What's doing?"

"Not much, Libby. How's them young'uns?"

"Oh, they're—" Right then, something crashed in the background and Libby sighed. "Boys."

I snickered. "Well, you know what they say."

"Boys will be boys." The words was said on a sigh made half of love and half of exasperation. "But you didn't call to talk about family."

"Sorry, cuz, but you're right. This is business." I give her the nickel version of Sophie's disappearance and shared Missy's concerns. The ring, I left out. I had no idea how to explain it, for one, but for another, I weren't rightly sure I should tell anybody else about it. When the explanation ran down, I said, "I was hoping I could borrow your painter nose to help track Sophie down."

"Sure," she said right off. "Not tonight. I know she's missing, but Elijah is over at Johnny's and I don't have a babysitter."

The hairs on the back of my neck stood straight up. Something was off in her voice, and it'd gone off right around the time she mentioned my grandpappy's name. "What's wrong with Johnny?"

"Oh, just a little heart trouble. Nothing to worry about."

Hurt sliced through me quicker'n spit. I was his granddaughter, dang it all, and his closest kin. If anybody was gonna worry about him, ort'n it be me?

"I'm sorry, Sunny," Libby said. "He didn't want me to tell you anything. For some reason, he's got this notion you'll make him go to an old folks' home."

"I'd sure make him go to the hospital," I said, kindly hot. "But I ain't putting him in one of them places. Do you know what they do to people in them retirement homes?"

Libby laughed of a sudden. "I told him you'd say something like that, but he's born of the woods. He's not ready to leave them yet."

That calmed me down a mite, enough for me to see through the red haze I hadn't even known was clouding my vision. "You tell that ol' coot I'll be over to see him soon as I get a minute."

And he might be sorry to see me coming, dang his stubborn hide.

Me and Libby chatted for a minute more, then said our goodbyes. Soon as we did, I texted Terry and told him we'd be over the next day, and tacked on a reminder for him to let me know if they found anything tonight, even if he didn't think it meant nothing. The least little clue might help, and he might walk right by it without even knowing it.

3

Riley come in about six that evening, just as I was pulling the meatloaf outta the oven. He sniffed real big and grinned as he dropped a large, brown envelope on my desk. "Something smells good."

I took one look at the grime coating his britches and said, "You ain't getting a bite 'til you wash up."

He shrugged off his coat and hung it by the door, then he stalked toward me and lifted me into a big ol' hug. He buried his face in my throat and sniffed again, and said, "You smell good enough to eat. Maybe I'll just have you instead."

I smacked his shoulders, playful like. "Get on with you now."

"One of these days," he muttered, and set me down by the stove. "Back in a jiff."

I clucked my tongue at him, but that didn't keep me from admiring his backside as he sauntered away from me.

Five minutes later, we sat down at the kitchen table and tucked into a plate of good ol' fashioned comfort food, some of Riley's favorites. I let him eat for a while. No sense burdening him with my load 'til he filled his belly.

And that took at least a full plate. Soon as he sat down with his second, he said, "What's this about missing kids?"

"I don't know yet," I admitted. "A little girl went missing over in Hiawassee. Terry Whitehead's daughter."

Riley went stiff as a board, poised with a forkful of mashed potatoes halfway to his mouth. He set it down careful on his plate, dabbed at his mouth with his napkin, and when he looked up at me, his hazel eyes glowed hot and bright. "You're doing a job for Terry Whitehead."

I set my own fork down and tried for reasonable. "I'm doing what I can to find Henry's baby sister."

"No," Riley said, and his voice was flat and hard as a granite cliff.

"No, what?"

"You're not helping him."

I about gaped at him. "A little girl is missing, Riley. She been lost in the woods for days now. It's January and cold out, if you ain't noticed, and the police done give up on her."

Riley glanced away and the muscles in his jaw worked, then he turned a hot glare on me. "I don't care. I don't want that son of a bitch anywhere near you."

My temper sparked, and I throwed my napkin down by my plate, so mad of a sudden, I coulda spit fire. "Riley Treadwell, you should be ashamed of yourself. Sophie ain't her daddy, but she sure is close enough to Henry for me to worry over her. I'm hunting her down, or trying my darnedest, and there ain't nothing you nor anybody else can do to stop me."

"Oh, yeah?"

"Yeah!"

He throwed down his own napkin, and danged if temper didn't color his cheeks. "Fine. You go help him out, but whenever you have to see him, I'd damn well better be there with you."

I sat back in my chair, and I did gape at him then. "What in tarnation? I ain't never needed no chaperone to do my dadgum job."

"Then it's about time you started," he said, his words as hot as his glare. "I'm sick of worrying about you, and I'm sick of worrying about some other guy snatching you away from me. You're my gal now and that's all there is to it. If Terry Whitehead wants you back, he'll have to go through me to get you."

Some of the anger drained outta me and I started to laugh. Well, of course, I was Riley's gal. That was all settled a while back, in my mind anyhow. "That's plumb silly."

"It's not silly for a man to not want a piece of trash sniffing around his woman."

"Now, look here, Riley. Ain't nobody sniffing around me but you."

A dangerous glint entered his eyes and he leaned close. "Well, I'm gonna make damn sure of that."

Before I could say spit, he pushed back from the table and stood up, and I recognized that glint in his eyes. Riley had loving on his mind. In the mood he was in, weren't no tender lover coming to kiss me, but a riled-up man running on temper. We ain't never had sex before, not all the way. Playing and touching and kissing, sure, but not full on sex. One of us was bound to get hurt if I let him near me in that mood, probably me, though I knowed he'd never hurt me of a purpose.

But if he did, I'd lose him, lose the only man I ever come close to loving, and what'd I do then?

A knot of something close to sorrow pricked at me. Lose Riley? No, I couldn't stand that, not again, maybe not ever. Panicked, I stood up, too, and held out a hand. "Hold on a minute now, Riley. Don't go doing nothing foolish."

"I've been holding on, Sunshine," he said, real quiet and

kindly sad. "I've been holding on since we were just kids and I am goddamn well tired of it."

Quick as lightning, his hands shot out and grabbed my upper arms, then he yanked me to him and his mouth met mine in a kiss so hot, it singed the ends of my hair.

Danged if ever lick of sense in my addled brain didn't fly right outta the window. I melted into him and sorta hummed in the back of my throat, and he growled into my mouth and licked me, and that was it for me. My heart hammered against my chest, or maybe that was his heart thumping into mine, and I lifted my hands to his waist and held on for dear life as the world spun around us and resettled into a new orbit.

Riley eased back and murmured against my lips. "Tell me you're ready, baby."

I bit my lower lip, too dazzled by the moment to open my eyes. "Ready for what?"

Riley let go of my arms, and I dropped back on my heels, and his hands cupped the back of my head, tangling into my hair, and his mouth touched mine again and away we went, into that beautiful country where just me and him lived. He started walking, guiding me with the pressure of his hips against my stomach, pushing me so gently, I didn't know we'd left the kitchen 'til his hands dropped to the bottom of the long-sleeved t-shirt I was wearing and started tugging it up.

My eyes popped open and I blinked into the light illuminating my bedroom. "What're we doing in here?"

Riley laughed, soft and low, and I shivered as he tugged my shirt off over my head and throwed it into the laundry basket. His shirt went next, up and over his head, his eyes on mine the whole time, only they wasn't so spit fire mad now. They was warm and tender and so gentle, what starch was left in my spine plumb melted outta me and I plopped down on the edge of the bed.

"Oh," I said, and he laughed again and followed me down, pushing me flat on my back beneath him as the mattress's springs squeaked under the weight of me and him together.

His weight settled between my legs and he pressed butterfly kisses to my forehead, my nose, my cheeks. "Tell me you're ready."

My fingers curled against his bare back, and without thinking, I spread my thighs a little wider, accommodating his hips. "For sex?"

"To make love with me," he corrected gently. "We've waited so long, Sunny. Don't make me wait any more. Be my gal, the way you should've been all along."

There weren't nothing I could say to that. I drawed him down to me and kissed him instead, showing him what I couldn't say. Some mistakes haunt you for the rest of your life, but this didn't have to be one of 'em. Riley didn't have to be a regret no more. He didn't have to be the friend I'd lost, my only friend, really. We wasn't them kids and hadn't been in what seemed like forever. It was time to let that past go and forge something new, something strong and whole and good.

It was time for me to trust him.

His thumbs stroked my cheeks, then he broke the kiss and stared down at me, as serious as I ever seen him. "Are you sure you're ready?"

I hefted out a huge sigh. "For crying out loud, Riley. Just come here already."

He laughed and touched his mouth to mine. Next thing I knowed, we was both naked as the day we was born. He slid into me, slow and easy, and he breathed my name on a reverent whisper, and it was a long, long time before we come up for air again.

IF WE COME DOWN to Earth, I didn't feel the descent. One minute Riley and me was floating through the heavens, joined together so well, my heart near about burst from it, and the next, seemed like, he rolled onto his side, taking me with him, and our skin was sweat slick and neither one of us could catch a good breath.

"Fuck, Sunny," he said, then he laughed and kissed my throat, and he slid outta me, leaving me so empty, I nearly cried.

I swallowed it down and aimed for my normal smart alec self. "Yup, I think that's what we did."

He snorted out a laugh against my skin, then nipped me with his sharp teeth. "Give me a minute and we can do it again."

"I'm still trying to figure out what brought the first round on."

His mouth stilled on my throat. He flopped over onto his back and throwed a forearm over his eyes. I slid my hand up his chest and placed my palm over his racing heart, happy just to be with him for once. It's not like I was waiting on an answer. I didn't really need one. It was nice to lay there with him and just *be* for a while.

After a minute, though, he muttered, "Jealousy."

I traced small circles through the sweat coating his chest, and finally mustered the energy to respond. "Of what?"

"He was your first lover."

I about swallowed my tongue, I was so shocked. Woke me right up, it did. "He weren't never my lover, Riley. We had sex once, and it weren't nothing to write home about."

"Once was enough."

Henry popped into my head. Yeah, Riley was right. Once was enough, and while what come after had been hard to live with, as soon as Henry arrived, ever single regret I had about giving myself to that wiener Terry fled like wildlife in front of a raging inferno.

I loved Henry with all my bitty heart and I wouldn'ta traded him for nothing. Sure did miss him, though, him and his Dumbo ears and that snaggle toothed grin of his and the way his dark eyes shone up at me, filled with so much love, it overflowed into me and filled me up, too.

That weird voice hissing at me the last time I visited his

memorial up the hill come to me, and I shoved it away, even as the little niggle of fear it'd planted took root and growed among the love.

"I wish I'd known him," Riley said. "Henry. I wish I'd had time with him."

I glanced up at Riley. He'd moved his arm and was looking down at me, and I smiled and touched a finger to his chin. "Me, too."

His eyes took on a certain gleam. "We're still young."

"Uh, yeah, we are. Why?"

Riley laughed and squeezed me tight. "Give me a minute."

I obligingly let him up and watched him walk into the bathroom, then I stared up at the ceiling pondering his words. We sure was young, but what did that have to do with anything? I sworn, that boy'd done befuddled me, I reckon, or maybe the sex had done me in. It'd been a long time since I'd done the deed, and never with a man like Riley.

That must be it, then. I was overcome by the quality of the man I was with.

I snickered into my elbow, tickled plumb pink by the notion. A minute later, Riley come out and nudged me onto my stomach, and danged if he didn't slide into me right then and there.

I twisted around and glanced over my shoulder at him. "Already?"

"Oh, yeah. You have no idea." He thrust into me, kindly languid, like we had all the time in the world and he intended to use ever bit of it. "Do you like to ski?"

My brain tried to shift gears from sex to conversation, and thudded against a hard wall of *no way, no how*. I buried my face in the bedspread and arched my back into his thrusts, and managed a muffled, "What?"

"Skiing. We could go up to Boone this weekend."

He shifted to the side and his hand snuck between me and the mattress and started rubbing on something mighty interesting. Truth be told, I lost track of the conversation right about then, what with drowning in all the pleasure he was giving me, and who could blame me? Riley sure did know a thing or two about pleasing a woman. I shoulda been jealous, but I didn't rightly have the brain power for that neither.

"I can rent you some equipment," he continued, like he weren't lighting ever cell of my body up like a Christmas tree. "Better, I'll buy you what you need. A ski jacket, at least."

That caught my attention real quick. I stopped moving and jabbed my elbow back into his ribs none too gentle. "You're gonna do what?"

"Buy you a ski jacket, maybe some skis, if you like it enough." He laughed into my nape and caught my elbow, holding it gentle but firm, likely 'cause I kept trying to elbow him. "Damn, Sunny. You're a hellion in bed."

Hurt hit me so hard, tears welled up in my eyes. I jerked my elbow free and thrashed around good, trying to buck him off, and he countered ever thing I done and stayed right where he was, still in me, and it was awful, just plumb awful having him in me when he said such a thing, and done such a thing.

Finally, the fight wore off me and I lay beneath him, panting hard. A sob escaped, though I woulda rather died than let it out voluntarily, and he stiffened on top of me and muttered, "Oh, my God. You're crying. What the hell?"

"Get off me," I said, and he did, soon as the words was out of my mouth, then I curled into a ball, facing away from him.

His hand fell on my shoulder and he curled around me, spooning me for all the world like he was trying to protect me. "What is it, baby? What's wrong?"

I squeezed my eyes shut and bit my lip against the hurt wadded up inside me, and my dang fool mouth opened up and spake anyhow. "I ain't no whore."

"What? When did I say you were a whore?"

"You was gonna buy me a ski jacket!"

A confused laugh sputtered out of him. "Well, yeah, I was thinking about it. I mean, it's pretty damn cold in Boone and I know your jacket's not warm enough to ski in."

Why did he have to sound so reasonable after what he done? "You can't buy me, Riley."

"For fuck's sake, Sunny. Is that what this is about?" He rolled away from me and muttered a long string of curses under his breath, then he heaved out a huge sigh and when he spoke again, his voice was tight and even. "Let's get one thing straight right now. You're my girlfriend. We're supposed to do things together. I'm supposed to do things *for* you, like get you a goddamn ski jacket, if that's the way I want to spend my money. I'm not trying to buy you off and I have never, not for one single, solitary second, ever thought you were a whore. Ever. Got it?"

That stopped my hurt dead in its tracks. I rolled over onto my back and looked at him where he lay flat on his back with both hands covering his face. My fool heart started remembering how good Riley been to me and how he never treated me no way but right, even when I was mean as a striped snake to him.

Like right about now.

If I coulda sunk through the Earth and out t'other side again, I think I woulda. How could one woman be that stupid? Yet here I was, acting like there weren't a lick of sense in my brain.

Real tentative like, I reached out a hand and rested it on his elbow. "I know I'm your gal, Riley."

"Then why are you always...? Fuck." A couple more curses erupted outta him, but not so harsh now, and he dropped his hands and stared up at the ceiling. "You've been my gal since that day we first met."

For some reason, that put a smile on my face. "We was just young'uns then."

"Yeah? Well, that's just too bad." He reached out and pulled me against his side and sighed into my crown. "You could try a saint's patience."

The way I figured it, I just had. I wrapped myself around him and kissed his chest. "I know. I'm real sorry for that."

"Thinking you're a whore." He huffed out another humorless laugh. "God, Sunny. Why would you even?"

Because that's the way I'd always been treated.

I squeezed my eyes tight against the thought. "I'll do better."

"No, baby," he said, real gentle. "There's nothing wrong with you, except maybe that you always think the worst of me."

"I don't, Riley," I said, but I sure could see how he'd thunk it. "I don't share my biscuits with just anybody, ya know."

He started chuckling then and ended up laughing so hard, he lost his breath. I propped myself up on one elbow and just watched him, and soon, my own mouth found a smile and I started laughing, and we laughed hard 'til he found his senses again and ushered us both into a shower.

4

That night, me and Riley settled on a compromise of sorts. I sure as tootin' weren't gonna wait around 'til it was convenient for him to leave work so's I could go do my job. On t'other hand, t'weren't nothing for me to text him and let him know I was headed over to the Whiteheads' to do some hunting for poor little Sophie. That satisfied his manly pride, and we went on about our evening the way we usually done, only with a lot more smooching and carrying on.

He spent the night, which he done before, but what come before in my bed weren't nothing compared to what happened that night. Riley wore me plumb out, or maybe I wore him out. Either way, we eventually fell asleep and slept like the dead 'til he snuck outta my bed at the cock's first crow so he could run home and clean up on his way to work.

Me, I snuggled into his pillow and fell back to sleep, and stayed that way 'til a light knock hit the front door. I pried one eye open and measured the thin light poking against the blinds. Nope, weren't time to get up yet.

The door squeaked open and a right proper voice called, "Sunny?"

I sighed. Well, dang. If it'd been anybody but Missy, I woulda stayed right where I was, playing sleep. For dang sure, I was giving Riley a key so he could lock up when he left.

"Be right there," I hollered as I threw off the covers and shivered in the chilly air.

A few minutes later, I was mostly dressed and plodding down the hallway. Missy was standing at the kitchen counter, measuring coffee grounds into the clean filter already stuffed into the coffee maker.

"Morning," I said, and plopped into a chair at the kitchen table.

"Good morning, dear."

Missy finished her task, then glided to the table and sank into a chair beside me. Her hair was twisted into two thick braids today, one on either side of her chin. She wore one of Fame's cast-off flannel shirts and an old pair of jeans, and for once, she had boots on, like as not 'cause it was colder'n a witch's tit outside.

Dark circles marred the creamy skin under her violet eyes. I studied them hard for a minute, then said, "You ok?"

Her gaze drifted away from me and fixed on some distant point only she could see, and her hands twitched into a knot in her lap. "Has the ring issued another warning?"

"Yesterday at the Whiteheads'." Real quick, I outlined what'd happened, how the ring warmed against my chest ever time I hit a certain point, and how I thought that point mighta lined up with a spot between there and wherever Sophie wandered off to. "I picked up some maps yesterday and spent some time familiarizing myself with the terrain, memorizing landmarks, that sorta thing."

She nodded and sorta hummed under her breath.

I waited for her to speak, and finally, my patience wore

through, or maybe the smell of coffee perking touched off a weak spot. "You wanna tell me what's going on with that ring now?"

Her lips parted and her eyes refocused on me, and dang me, I'm nigh on certain she woulda spilled her guts right then and there if somebody hadn't knocked on the door. A second later, Libby stuck her head into the living room, spotted me, and slid on into the room, grinning hello.

I left them two to it and snuck back to the bathroom for a quick shower. No way was I going into the woods with my cousin and her sniffer when I smelled like Riley and sex.

WHEN I COME back into the kitchen, Missy was gone and Libby was sitting at the kitchen table with a cup of fresh brewed coffee smack dab in front of her, wiping her nose with a tissue.

I tugged out a chair and sat down, boots in hand. "You ok?"

She nodded, tucked the tissue into one fist, sipped her coffee. Sneezed good and swiped her nose.

"Bless you." I slipped my feet into my boots and bent over to tie 'em. "Want some breakfast? I can whip something up real quick."

She tapped her nose with the tip of one finger. "It'll be better if I wait until after, but I don't mind waiting while you eat."

"Not too hungry," I admitted. "I was gonna fix a coupla sandwiches to take with us. I know changing takes a lot outta you."

"It does."

I finished tying my boots and stomped 'em for good measure, and a few minutes later, out the door we went, Libby with a thermos of coffee, me with a cooler full of sandwiches for her, and both of us carrying our own coffee in thermal mugs.

It was a good drive over to the Whiteheads'. I didn't get to chat much with women my age, save when I run into my gal pal BobbiJean, and my instincts about Libby when I learnt how we was kin was dead on: Me and her was destined to be good friends, the way close cousins should be.

Besides. I enjoyed hearing her go on about the young'uns and family life, so I prodded her along them ends and lapped up ever story she was willing to share. If a niggle or two of envy wormed its way into my heart, I ignored it. I had my own feller now. I weren't stupid enough to hope for more. Sometimes it was nice to dream on it though.

Terry's battered work truck was gone when me and Libby pulled into the driveway and parked. We hadn't done more'n cut off the engines and open the doors when Ellie walked out carrying a swaddled infant. She waited there on the porch with us, rocking and swaying in time to some tune only she could hear.

Me and Libby walked up the neat little pathway running from the parking lot to the porch steps, and I introduced one to t'other.

Libby, being the friendly sort, reached out and run a finger along the edge of the blanket, right where the babe's left arm would be. "Boy or girl?"

"A boy." Ellie smiled and obligingly shifted the blankets away from the babe's face, revealing a sleeping infant with a crown of fine, downy hair and ears jutting out on either side of his round, little face. "He ain't a month old. Come close to being a Christmas babe."

I clucked my tongue. Poor gal, having her daughter disappear on her while she was still recovering from childbirth. "He's a handsome feller. What's his name?"

Ellie's smile faded a mite and turned wistful, and she glanced down at her son. "Terrence Henry, after his daddy and his big brother. I hope you don't mind, Sunny."

Tears popped into my eyes and something hit me right in the chest, something like pride and sorrow and love all rolled into one, and I couldn't resist no more. I held my arms out and accepted little Terrence Henry from his mama and cuddled him close, cooing to him the way I done to my own little Henry so many years back.

Libby draped an arm around my shoulder and squeezed, and I said, "Them ears must run in the family," and we all laughed, startling the poor little tyke awake. He let out a wail like the very devil'd bit him good, and I give him over to his mama, but not before sneaking in a tiny smooch on his smooth forehead.

"I'll be right back with something of Sophie's," Ellie said, then she slipped inside the house and Terrence Henry's cries receded.

Soon as the door shut on her, Libby pulled me into a full hug. "It's ok, Sunny."

"I know," I said into her hair, but I held on for a minute anyhow. My Henry was dead, and God above knowed I missed him ever day. His passing left a hole in my heart, a hole nobody else was ever gonna fill, but at least a small part of him lived on in his bitty brother and, God willing, the sister me and Libby was gonna find come Hell or high water.

I WAITED on the porch for Ellie while Libby went back to the car and shimmied outta her clothes for the change. It didn't take long for either one, and about ten minutes later, me and Libby was walking away from the house along the line Missy's ring'd pointed out to me, Libby on four furry paws.

The ring was warm against my chest under my jacket, though not hot like it'd got when Terry first told me about Sophie. I done give Libby a good smell of the stuffed animal Sophie slept with. Somebody'd been smart enough to bag it in a humongous, zip top, plastic bag. All I'd had to do was open it and let Libby stick her snout in, then I'd closed it back up, sealing Sophie's scent inside in case we, or somebody else, needed it again.

Libby set a slow pace. Her head was up, snout testing the air, and I had the feeling she was sniffing for something other'n Sophie's scent, or something in addition to it.

I was content to walk alongside her with the fingers of one hand touching her crown between her ears. Ever once in a while, something stretched between us, like a thread what hadn't been spun well or tight enough, and beyond that, flashes of emotion and sensation come to me, little flickers of what I suspected she was seeing or feeling.

The forest outside the Whiteheads' was open at first, and it was pretty obvious somebody'd taken the time to clear out the undergrowth and saplings. Wooden stairs wound around a huge poplar, up, up, up 'til they hit the bottom of a tree house perched among the bare branches.

Sophie's, I reckoned, set there by Terry or one of his kin.

I shook off the pang of sorrow I hadn't expected and walked side by side with Libby, deeper into the woods. It was thicker here. The smell of decaying leaves, dimmed by winter's cold, tickled my nose, and laurel tangled together among the trees, at first in clusters of one or two young plants, later in whole patches stretching well over my head. Their leaves was long and oblong and glossy green, dark like the forest here, where even in winter sunlight seldom pierced the canopy towering some fifty feet or more above my head.

Beyond, through the nude trunks of trees large and small, I caught sight of another house, Terry's folks, I reckoned, but other'n that and a coupla trails beat into the ground by feet animal or human, not much else. It was cold out, that's for sure, and my bare fingers chilled and reddened the longer we walked, along with my nose and the tips of my ears.

Which is what I got for leaving my hat and gloves in the car. For once, I envied Libby her black fur coat.

I don't know how long we walked, or how far, but of a sudden, Libby's head shot down 'til the tip of her nose nigh

34

on touched the ground. I crouched beside her, careful to draw my hands back outta her way. "What is it, cuz?"

She snuffled along the ground, swung her head around to me, then nudged the bag holding Sophie's stuffed animal. Obligingly, I knelt and opened it up for her and let her get another good whiff. That was all she needed. Soon as she pulled her head away, she twisted around and broke into a fast trot. A curse popped outta my mouth as I shot up and tried to close the bag's zip top and run after her at the same time.

Oh, well. Another quarter for my cussing jar.

Away we went, me trailing her by a good twenty feet, her loping through the woods around straggly jack pines and bushy cedars and a maple so big around, me'n her both couldn'ta got our arms around it.

Right about then, Missy's ring went from warm to scorching hot, and the thrill of the hunt tweaked my blood. My vision went a little wonky at the edges, like I was in a fishbowl or something and water blurred the peripherals, and a connection more powerful'n anything I ever felt grabbed hold of me and rooted me in a feeling I'd only had a coupla times.

Libby purred and it sounded almost like a laugh, only it filtered to me through my ears and that connection. I glanced up, and there she was, waiting on the trail ahead of me. Soon as I caught up, she leapt into a run, faster now, and I pumped my arms and legs, running like I never run before.

Wind whipped by me, streaming through my hair, stinging my eyes as my heart thumped and my blood raced and a glorious freedom lifted me from the mundane into the sacred.

I was the forest, and the forest was me, and Libby was there, too, separate yes, but a part of me so deep, for a minute, I couldn't sort the two of us out.

And there was a smell there, too, a sharp tang that tasted red and dark on my tongue, like blood, but not, and somewhat familiar in the way it twined about me.

The ring sang higher and stronger, ebbing in time with the tang's strength, and it hit me in some distant part of my mind that the ring knew that tang, knew it, loved it, craved it, and if I was smart, I'd keep the ring far, far away from whatever the source of that tang was.

One minute we was running along fine, rejoicing in the thrill of the hunt. The next, Libby skidded to a stop and tumbled head over tail along the forest floor, landing in a heap inside a thatch of huckleberries and brambles.

I thudded to a stop, laughing in spite of myself, from the run or the sight of Libby all tangled up in the undergrowth, I couldn't tell.

She freed herself with a dignified shrug and padded back to the spot that'd tripped her up. It was flat and a little muddy. I glanced up, noted the gap in the trees above where rain mighta leaked through as Libby prowled around the area, a low growl deep in her throat. She sneezed, drawing my attention back to her, and soon as I glanced down, she shook her head back and forth.

I knelt there and sifted through the leaves, but try as I might, I didn't notice a single thing, not a footprint or a broken branch or nothing else what'd clue me or Libby either one in on what'd happened at that spot.

We tried a few minutes more, then Libby nudged my legs and pointed me back toward the Whiteheads'. I stumbled along beside her, worn out from the chase or the loss of the connection with Libby or the disappointment of not finding Sophie, or maybe all three.

5

Ꮎy the time we got back to the car, I was sweaty and grumpy and plumb wore out. My belly growled right then, protesting its empty state with a rumble loud enough to wake the dead. I plodded over the IROC, opened the passenger door so Libby could hop in and change. The house's front door creaked open right as her tail whipped around the door and into the car.

I glanced up, and there was Ellie, standing on the top step in socked feet with her hands tucked into her back pockets and her hair pulled into a tidy ponytail. I shook my head and trudged over to her, leaving the IROC's door open, but if Ellie saw Libby's tail, it didn't faze her one bit.

"Find anything?" she said.

I shook my head and handed her the bagged stuffed animal, then leaned a hip against a newel at the bottom of the stairs. "Trail stopped cold, far as we can tell."

"That's what Terry and them said," she murmured as her gaze shifted away from mine and focused on something in the distance behind me. "Trail went cold. No wonder the police give up. If the hounds can't sniff out my poor Sophie, what good are people?"

I didn't have an answer for her and that's the pure plumb truth. "We're not giving up."

"Me, neither."

But her words didn't sound near as firm as they shoulda, and that worried me a mite.

Libby hollered at me just then, and I bade Ellie farewell on a promise to keep trying. Soon as my butt hit the driver's seat and I shut the door on the cold, Libby turned toward me in the seat.

"Did you smell it?" she asked.

I cranked the engine and listened to the hum. "Smell what?"

"The man. Pop the hatch, would you?"

I obliged and Libby got out. A minute later, the hatch slammed shut and she slid into her seat and set the cooler full of sandwiches on her lap. I backed up and turned around, pointed the IROC toward home, and give her some time to fill her belly. Lord knows, she'd used up enough energy out on the trail, enough for three of the heaping full ham and cheese sandwiches I made for her that morning.

After the first one was washed down with some coffee, she sighed and leaned back in the seat and closed her eyes. "The man."

"What about him?"

"You didn't smell him?" She placed her hand over mine on the steering wheel, and it came back to me, that red and dark tang what'd tickled my senses. "Magic."

So that's what that was. "Not any magic I know."

"Me, neither. It's..." She squinched up her nose and her hand fell off mine, and at last she said, "Foreign."

I nodded, though I hadn't the foggiest idea what she

meant.

"And another magic, too, something like Missy's."

My foot slipped off the accelerator and I gawped at her. "What do you mean, like Missy's? Missy ain't magic. She's just a hiker what got lost and wound up on Fame's doorstep one day."

Libby huffed out a laugh. "Is that what she told you?"

"That's what I know."

"Well, she's magic. I can't believe you can't sense it. Why do you think I sneeze every time me and her are in the same room together?"

Real careful like, I stuck my foot to the accelerator and sped back up to the speed limit. "I just thought it was allergies or something."

"Allergies is probably a good word for it. Two different kinds of magic, panther and..." She hesitated again, then shook her head and dug out another sandwich. "Foreign, but not like the man I smelled."

I give her a minute to wolf down the second sandwich whilst all this talk about magic wound around inside me. Missy I'd deal with when I got home, though as much as I trusted Libby, I thought her nose was off there.

Still, that left them other two magics. Two people, I reckoned, one with the dark scent I'd picked up and t'other with...what?

"Like Missy's, but not," Libby said around a mouthful of sandwich. She swallowed and washed it down with coffee, then added, "Sorry. I picked up what you were thinking."

That shocked me good. "All of it?"

"Just the feelings. Worry over Missy, wondering about what we'd found." Libby shrugged and polished off the sandwich. "Can we stop at the McDonald's we passed on the way here?"

"Any one you want, or if you'd rather, there's a meat and three in Hayesville."

"Perfect," Libby said, and I sworn a purr underscored

the word.

"So them two magics you sniffed out?"

"The man was with Sophie. The other was only at that one spot."

"And nothing beyond it?"

Libby shook her head and pulled out the third sandwich I'd made her. "It's like a hole opened up in the earth and swallowed all three of them."

A deep foreboding knotted my stomach up and the ring pinged, it what'd gone stone cold on me by the time we returned to the Whiteheads'. I hit the turn signal and headed toward Hayesville, and put all of it outta my mind. Time enough for pondering once our bellies was filled and Libby was on her way home, but once that was done? Yeah, me and Missy was gonna have a us a little talk about this magic Libby said she possessed, assuming I could pin her down long enough to get her to spill the beans.

A COUPLA HOURS LATER, I parked in my driveway in front of the trailer and said my goodbyes to Libby. She hugged me good and hurried on her way, and I trudged into my roost, yawning up a storm.

Lordy, but tracking down young'uns took the gumption out of a body.

On the way into the kitchen, my gaze landed on the snapshot Terry'd left of him and Sophie, and my hurt squeezed tight in my chest. Days missing now, out in the cold, only I was nigh on certain she weren't in the cold no more.

How could three people just disappear in the middle of the woods?

I dumped the cooler and thermal mug on the kitchen counter, then detoured into the bedroom and flopped out across the bed. Clean up could come later. I needed some shut eye, just a few minutes to make up for the long night with Riley and the long morning running through the woods...

A hound bayed in the distance.

Sophie run through the woods, her long brown curls bouncing around her shoulders. Snow drifted down around her, falling onto her down jacket, and leaves crunched under her booted feet.

She glanced over her shoulder and smiled at me, and her eyes was so like Henry's, my heart cried out.

Something blotted the sun, casting a blight over her, and I glanced up. A great shadow crept across the sky, like a giant thundercloud rolling in, carrying with it an icy darkness.

Sophie laughed and raced ahead of me, and fear gripped me. I reached out for her, trying to grab hold, trying to save her from that evil blanketing the land, but she slipped through my fingers and was lost, alone in the woods surrounded by that shadow.

I called to her again and again. My voice echoed back to me, carrying a dozen other names along the wind, names I never heard or seen before, names I never ken.

A twig cracked nearby and I whirled around, my heart thumping hard in my chest. Something pierced the darkness, a tiny light low to the ground. I dropped down and crept toward it on all fours, and the light separated into two and jumped toward me and become the eyes of a painter, and recognition hit.

Sunny, Johnny Walkingstick whispered. *Come home.*

I sat straight up in bed, eyes wide and blinking, and slapped a palm over my pounding heart. Shoulda knowed better'n to nap during the day. It'd never agreed with me, nor me with it, but this'un beat just about all I ever seen.

I shook my head, trying to shed the oily feel of evil. The only thing I accomplished was giving myself a pounding headache. I pinched my temples between fingers and thumb and rubbed good.

One thing was for certain. The next time my grandpa needed me, he'd better call me on the dadgum phone instead of hollering at me in my dreams.

I HOPPED IN THE SHOWER and cleaned up, then stomped to my desk, still het up over that dadgum dream.

Which reminded me. I backtracked and dropped a quarter in my cussing jar, grabbed some water and an aspirin, and plopped down behind my desk, my gaze glued to Terry and Sophie smiling outta that picture.

Hang it all, there was only so much a woman could take. I swallowed down the pill and set my water aside, then folded the picture in half so only Sophie's image showed. Not a soul could blame me for not wanting to look on a man what'd done me wrong.

That envelope Riley brung from his daddy yesterday caught my eye next. I pulled it over, opened it up, and emptied it onto my desk. Weren't much there, truth be told. A few photocopies of police reports, looked like, and a piece of notebook paper with a note scrawled across it. I squinted at the blue ink for a minute and finally deciphered it.

This is all I could get in one day, it read. *Will have more soon. Keep me informed of your progress. Chip.*

I snorted out a laugh, torn between outrage and gratitude. He just had to go and order me around. Keep him informed indeed, like I was one of his deputies or something.

At least he'd kept his promise, or tried to anyhow, and that was good enough in my book.

I shuffled the photocopied pages into a pile and begun studying 'em, one at a time. The top most one was dated a month past and was from the Hayesville, North Carolina, police department, Hayesville being the seat of Clay County, where Terry and Ellie lived. Michael Earl Miller, aged eight years and four months, disappeared from his yard one afternoon after school. No traces found. His home was located in Warne. Likely he was the one Ellie had remembered.

The next one was from Towns County, Georgia, the next county south of Clay County and just west of where I lived. Isabella Amanda Stiwinter, aged seven years and nine months, was playing at a friend's house one Saturday afternoon just before Halloween. Her mama called her home for supper, only she never made it the half mile between the two houses. The trail cut through the woods and was searched heavily, but no traces of her was found.

The third and final sheet was dated some forty years past, long before I was born, and when I caught sight of the name, I slumped back in my chair, too surprised to look away.

Darren Wayne Treadwell, aged six years nearly on the dot, disappeared in the woods behind his family's home in the Bridge Creek area of Rabun County and was never found again.

I totted up the math in my head and landed on a near certain sum: Ten to one young Darren was Chip Treadwell's younger brother, one I never heard tale of.

That weren't the surprising part. The feud betwixt the Treadwells and the Carsons run more'n one generation back. Seeing as how I'd avoided all but the two Treadwells what was good to me, it weren't surprising I didn't know about Chip's baby brother going missing.

No, what was surprising was that the report was in there at all. What did Darren's disappearance have to do with Sophie's? How could they be connected when the two happened some four decades apart?

The answers to them questions remained stubbornly elusive, so I opened up my case notebook and jotted down notes about the two more recent disappearances, then added to my growing list of things I needed to research. I really needed to look through the local police departments' Facebook pages, but seeing as how I refused to buy a computer or a phone with Wi-Fi access, I'd have to make a special trip to the library to cross that one off my list.

I throwed down my pen and slapped my hands to my thighs. Hang it all, I really did need to break down and buy a laptop or something, but then I'd have to get the internet installed here. God alone knowed how much trouble that'd be.

I could just borrow Riley's.

An automatic denial rose in me, and I squashed it right good and hard. It was past time I started leaning on him for help. Not so much he done ever thing for me, no. Of course, not. But he'd be right happy to lend me his laptop ever once in a while, and weren't no harm in me using it. When my conscience started harping on me for borrowing too much, I could repay him with dinner or a massage or something. We could make it a fair trade.

By the time I finished chastising myself, I was grinning ear to ear thinking of all the fair trading me and Riley could do. Some of my thinking touched on the naughty. When Riley heard about it, and I'd be sure to give him ever sparkling detail, it'd tickle him pink and then some, or my name weren't Sunshine Rainbow Walkingstick.

6

Since I was just up that way, or close enough, I decided Johnny could wait another day or two. I did text Libby and ask her to pass a message along for me saying as much, and she texted back with a promise to tell the old goat.

My words, not hers. She was a mite more respectful toward my grandpa than I was ever gonna be.

By the time I finished making my notes and doing what I could get done from home, it was after four. I tidied my desk, chose a record outta my daddy's collection (Whitesnake's self-titled album), and stood in the doorway of Henry's room as David Coverdale belted out the opening lines of "Crying in the Rain."

It was getting harder and harder for me to come in here. I crossed my arms over my boobs and leaned against the doorframe as I stared at the remnants of my boy's life. His bed, covered in a red and blue plaid quilt what used to be Trey's. The drawings pinned to the peeling wallpaper above the dinged, wooden headboard. The tiny chest of drawers painted cornflower blue with white clouds blotted up the sides. I done that myself in an earnest attempt to give my boy something besides me what was his and his alone.

If he'da lived a few more years, maybe he woulda knowed Sophie. Maybe his baby brother woulda bore a different name and they woulda growed up together, the way siblings should. The way me and Trey and Gentry did, though I was cousin to them and not sister.

That weren't the life fate'd had in store for my Henry, God rest him. If I could help it, Sophie weren't gonna meet the same heartbreaking end.

'Less she already had.

Chills broke out on my arms under my shirt and I rubbed 'em hard. Was there any help for Sophie, what with her trail going cold as the snow in my dream?

I shivered again and shoved myself off the doorframe and into Henry's room. I had a coupla hours before I was needed elsewhere. Might as well make good use of the time and scrub this corner of my roost. It'd been shut up for years, but that didn't stop cobwebs and dust from gathering, and if there was two things I didn't care to have living under my roof, it was cobwebs and dust.

Riley stomped into the house a good hour later, carrying the evening's chill and a dusting of fresh snow on his canvas jacket. "Honey, I'm home," he hollered, and I fluffed a pillow down on Henry's freshly washed sheets and grinned.

That Riley.

I went out and greeted him with a solid kiss. "You're early."

"I'm late." His fingers tightened on my hips and he kissed my forehead. "What time's supper?"

"We're eating at Fame's."

A longsuffering sigh burst outta him. "The things I do for you."

I laughed and fingered the buttons of his work shirt.

"You be real good and you can do 'em again after."

"Now there's a promise a man can live for."

I reckoned so, though I wouldn't tell him such. No need agreeing with him all the time. Instead, I took his hand and lead him into the bedroom, and while we didn't have time for much other'n cleaning up, we made the most of it in the best way possible.

SEEING AS HOW it was freezing outside and the sun'd set, we bumped up to Fame's the long way in Riley's Range Rover. Me, I woulda humped it up the hill, flashlight in hand, but Riley weren't having none of that. We could go up in his SUV or not a'tall, and since my bellybutton was rubbing a hole in my spine, I weren't gonna argue with him.

Fame's trailer was lit up like a Christmas tree. Riley parked behind Trey's truck and cut off the engine. We'd just slid outta the seats into the brisk air when Gentry burst outta the front door onto the porch with the critter sitting proud and bold on his shoulder.

"Guess who's here?" he hollered.

"Besides me?" I hollered back.

Gentry grinned real big. "You's always here."

"So it's not me." I slid a side-eyed glance at Riley. "What about my feller?"

"C'mon, Sunny. Guess good."

Riley threaded his bare fingers through mine and grinned down at me. "Can I play?"

I shrugged a shoulder, which Riley took as consent.

"Santa Clause," he said.

Gentry shook his head and scowled. "He only comes on Christmas Eve, Riley. Don't you know nothing?"

I snickered and tugged Riley into a faster pace. "It's too cold to play guessing games in the cold."

We didn't need to for long nohow. Soon as we was inside, I saw exactly who'd come to dinner.

"Old Mother," I murmured.

She was sitting next to Trey on the couch, her forehead near about touching his while Missy bustled around Fame's brand of help in the kitchen. For once, Old Mother was dressed in street clothes, jeans and a chunky sweater the color of holly berries, and even had on a nice pair of leather boots.

How Trey'd got her into shoes was beyond me, but I was thankful I weren't the one having to drag her in outta the cold.

Trey glanced up and shot me a warning glare, then proceeded to ignore my blunder, thank heavens. "Riley, have you met Mary Alice?"

"I haven't had the pleasure." Riley shrugged off his coat and hung it beside the door, then stepped forward and shook Old Mother's hand. "I'm Riley Treadwell, Sunny's boyfriend."

Old Mother withdrew her hand and folded it together with her other one in her lap, around one of Trey's paws, and said, in her normal South Georgia accent, "I've seen you, Riley."

"Er," Riley said.

"I'll explain later," I muttered. "Good to see you, Mary Alice."

"Sunny." She tilted her head to the side and her eyes unfocused a bit, like she was looking at something beyond me. "You have trouble."

I glanced at Trey, scuffed my feet against the welcome mat. Of course, she knowed about Sophie. Old Mother was a seer and a right good'un, but one look at Trey and I figured I'd best keep my mouth shut about it, else he'd rake me over the coals but good. I weren't up for that right then and I sure didn't wanna ruin all Missy's hard work.

"It's nothing I can't handle," I said at last.

Missy bustled into the room, Fame hot on her heels. "What can't you handle?"

"The, uh." I floundered around for an appropriate explanation and settled on, "Kids."

"Oh," Missy said. "That can wait until after we eat. Wash up, Gentry, and put Hob back in his cage. Supper's ready."

Gentry grumped a bit, but back into the cage the critter went and into the bathroom my cousin went to wash his hands. Trey stood up with Mary Alice and lead her into the kitchen behind Fame. Riley headed that way, and nearly run over Mary Alice when she stopped and slipped her hand out of Trey's and hung back with me.

"Trey doesn't want me seeing for you anymore," she whispered.

I glanced at his retreating back and a twinge of sympathy hit me. Poor feller didn't know what he'd gotten into when he started courting Mary Alice. No need for me to make it harder on him. "It's ok, honey. Don't you worry none, you hear?"

"You need to know things, Sunny. Something's coming."

"Something's always coming," I said, gentle as I could. "That don't mean you gotta get involved."

Her hand snaked out and latched onto mine. Her fingernails dug into my skin, and for a minute, her eyes went dark and round and her voice slipped into the hoodoo tones of a foretelling. "The red calls to you, Sunshine. The teardrop draws near and it seeks her return. Power likens unto power."

"Mary Alice," Trey said, his voice sharp as a fresh honed knife.

She dropped my hand and her eyes returned to normal, and so did her voice. "I'm fine, Trey, honey."

He glanced at me, his gaze as sharp as his voice. "See that you stay that way."

I shrugged at him. "I didn't start it."

"No, I did," Mary Alice said with a smile. "Just a minute, ok?"

Trey nodded and pivoted around on his heel back into the kitchen, though a frown stuck to his mouth the likes of which I never seen.

Mary Alice leaned toward me and lowered her voice to a

whisper. "Use the ring, Sunny."

My fingers touched the ring hanging on a chain under my shirt. "Use it how?"

"You'll know when the time comes." She patted my hand and her smile trembled away. "I'm sorry I can't be of more help. I could use the herbs for a proper seeing—"

I shook my head, interrupting her before she could rattle off things I didn't rightly wanna know. "None of that, now. Supper's waiting and Missy gets right prickly if we let her hard work spoil."

Mary Alice nodded and followed Trey to the table, but that troubled look she wore haunted me right through the evening meal and well into bedtime.

7

After a night of sound sleep, thanks to Riley's magic touch, and a quick phone call to Libby, I started the next morning off at the library in Clayton hunting through Facebook pages, beginning with the Towns County Sheriff's Department. I found the posts about Isabella Stiwinter going missing, including the Amber Alert and pleas from her family, and dutifully printed 'em out.

Soon as I had them in hand, I backtracked and checked out the Facebook pages of anybody what'd liked or commented on the posts about her, starting with her likely family members. I found her parents pretty quick. They shared a page and, ever once in a while, posted a heart wrenching picture of little Isabella out playing with her cousins and whatnot.

I sent 'em my phone number in a message, told 'em what was going on, and asked if me and Libby could poke around. I made a mental note to check back in on Facebook in a coupla days if I didn't hear back from 'em.

The rest of the commenters seemed to be family and friends. Not a single one stood out as unusual. I gathered up as much information as I could about each of 'em anyhow, ever thing from who was stepping out on who, to who was a-feuding and who weren't, to what their regular schedules was.

Nobody realized just how much a body could figure out about their personal lives by reading their Facebook page, and believe me, I gathered a lot of gossip that morning.

I figured out localities as best I could and wrote 'em down, then tapped into Google Maps and viewed the woods around the Stiwinters' house. Their address would go on my physical topographical map at the trailer, but for now, I just needed to see where they lived in relation to the Whiteheads.

I did the same with the Miller boy over in Warne, beginning with the Hayesville Police Department and the Clay County Sheriff's Office, and working my way out to family and friends, including sending a message to his parents. The father was a deputy. Other'n that, nobody seemed unusual or suspicious there neither, but it didn't hurt to check.

When I finished, there was maybe an hour left 'til lunch, so I scrolled down the various police departments' pages looking for more missing kids, then moved on to neighboring jurisdictions. I found four more young'uns going back a coupla months, spread out over northeast Georgia and southwestern North Carolina, all still missing, far as I could tell. That took up the rest of my time, but I made a note to check the upstate South Carolina and eastern Tennessee areas. We weren't that far from neither place. If somebody was ranging far and wide to abduct young'uns, and it seemed like they was, then it weren't out of the question they'd also be drifting across into them areas.

I had a quick bite to eat with Riley over at the Sunday Diner, then out of curiosity more'n anything, I headed to the Probate Court at the county courthouse, near the library, and flipped through the old newspapers in the vault from four decades past.

It didn't take long a'tall to find Darren Treadwell's obituary and the few little articles about his disappearance. The family was mentioned, of course, and the fact that he'd disappeared outta the yard while his older brother was inside finishing up some homework.

For a minute, I put myself in the Sheriff's shoes and imagined how awful he musta felt when he went outside and couldn't find his baby brother. Was that why he become a police officer, or had his brother's disappearance merely cemented Chip's role in the family business?

I shook my musings off, pulled out the tiny camera I'd brung along just in case, and photographed the articles and the dates they'd been published. Maybe Darren's disappearance had something to do with this latest rash of abductions and maybe it didn't, but it didn't hurt to keep track of my own research, did it?

TRUTH BE TOLD, it didn't take long to search through them old newspapers, and that was a good thing, seeing as how I was needed elsewhere that afternoon.

I jogged down the courthouse stairs from the second floor to the first and high stepped it through the lobby past a lone deputy manning the metal detector. When I hit the fresh air, a message popped into my phone from the Miller boy's mama. I checked it and answered back, then texted Libby one-handed as I slid behind the wheel of the IROC.

The day was cool, but fair, and the sun shone bright among the white streaks of jet exhaust crisscrossing the sky. I tuned the radio to a classic rock station out of Atlanta and pointed the IROC's nose down the same path I trod yesterday, heading toward Snowbird Cherokee territory.

Johnny was sitting out on the porch, corncob pipe clutched between his teeth, when I parked in his driveway.

Never mind that it was January and he weren't wearing no coat over his plaid shirt, this'un green and orange. The cold didn't make no never mind to him, I reckoned, or maybe he was just a stubborn ol' coot.

Me, I voted for the latter, but I bit my tongue around that thought and stomped up to the front porch like I had ever right to be there.

Shoot, I was his only kin now, what with Daddy and my grandma and the rest of his close kin having passed on at one point or another over the years, God rest 'em. The way I figured it, that give me all the rights I needed to poke my nose into his business, decades spent apart or not.

"Johnny," I said and plopped down in the rocking chair beside him.

He pulled the unlit pipe outta his teeth and nodded. "Pretty day for a visit."

"My foot." A good dose of starch coated my voice. I gritted my teeth, swallowed down a sharp retort as to how a man his age ortn't to be sitting on the porch with the mercury hovering under fifty degrees. "Libby says you was at the doctor for your heart."

"It's still a-ticking."

"Then what was you there for?"

He chomped down on the lip of his pipe and gnawed for a minute. A car drove down the street, slowing as it passed Johnny's, and the driver peered at us like she never seen a half-white woman sitting on a man's porch in the middle of Snowbird territory before. A jet screamed overhead, its roar distant, and two squirrels chittered at each other over an acorn under a giant oak.

Finally, he said, "Heart don't beat right, ain't since I was a boy."

"And you're just now telling me?"

"Your daddy knew." He puffed on the unlit pipe, withdrew it, and dropped his hand to the rocking chair's arm. "I woulda told you along and along."

"Along and along shoulda been before the dadgum thing broke and I had to visit your grave to say goodbye."

I clenched my lips together tight and rubbed a weary hand over my eyes. Lordy, but there weren't nothing like family to rile a body. Still, Johnny was family and about the only kin I had left on Daddy's side, outside the loads of Cherokee cousins I still hadn't met yet. And he was my elder and deserving of some respect. If nothing else, I could use a civil tongue when speaking to him.

I inhaled a deep breath, let it out real slow, and tried again. "I was worried about you, is all."

"Nothing to worry about." His foot pushed against the porch's wooden slats, rocking his chair back, and a sly grin stretched his mouth. "'Less you feel the need to make me one of them blueberry dump cakes. You ever con the recipe outta your cousin Libby?"

All the mad drained outta me and I laughed. "Libby ain't giving that recipe up to me nor you neither one, old man, but you just keep right on a-hoping."

"That's all a man's got when he gets to be my age, Sunny. Hope." His gaze fixed on something across the road. He stuck the pipe between his lips and his teeth clamped tight on it for a second. "There's a storm brewing, little one."

I gazed at the sky, blue and clear as a bell, and opened my mouth to retort as to how there weren't a cloud hanging out up there. Then that dream popped into my head, Sophie and darkness and painter eyes, and I snapped my mouth shut. Something was a-brewing, all right, or maybe it done got here. Weren't no way to know but to sit tight and wait it out.

Between the missing kids, Old Mother's oddities, and now Johnny's, seemed like whatever was headed toward us' was coming in mighty fast and hard. I weren't near enough ready for it, nor did I wanna talk on it to a man what had heart problems.

I cleared my throat and let my hands flop onto the arms of the rocking chair. "Riley sends his love," I said, then me and Johnny settled down for a good chat as the sun dropped toward the horizon. Time flew by like a crow pushed along by a good tailwind, and before I knowed it, Libby pulled into the driveway and my time with my daddy's daddy was up for one day.

8

Me and Libby headed out soon as she pecked my grandpa on the cheek and fussed at him 'til he went inside outta the cold. I'da loved to learn that trick, but we had young'uns to track and we was losing the light, or would if we didn't get our tails in gear.

Libby literally.

I snickered as I slid my seatbelt across my waist and switched the IROC's engine on.

Libby glanced up at me, her eyebrows raised. "What's so funny?"

"We're gonna lose the light if we don't get our tails in gear."

"Hardy har." She clicked her seatbelt into place, still half cattycorner to me. "I'm all yours until supper. Elijah's off this afternoon."

I twisted around in the seat and glanced at the road

behind us, checked the mirrors good, then backed carefully onto the road and outta Johnny's driveway. "Anything wrong at work?"

"Just slowing down. It's to be expected." She shrugged. "He's got Charlie with him now and is going to pick the boys up from basketball practice after school and take them shopping. Grocery shopping. They're making supper tonight."

I cut my eyes at her, trying real hard to hide my grin. "I bet that's gonna be a mess and a half to clean up."

"Oh, they're in charge of clean up, too. I told Elijah if I walked into the house and saw even a cushion out of place, they'd all be cleaning this weekend instead of going to basketball games."

"You're a wicked'un."

"You have no idea." She shook her head, though she was grinning about as big as I was. "Anyway, he said to ask you to come, and Riley, too, and not to take no for an answer. The boys barely get to see you."

A little hint of guilt cut through the happy. I swallowed it down and navigated toward the main road. It weren't hardly my fault I didn't meet my daddy's kin 'til a few months past and I weren't keen on dwelling on them sorrowful times right before going out on a hunt for a missing young'un.

Libby saved me, though, like she always done, and turned the conversation to Jacob and Wyatt's schooling and basketball and all the things her boys got up to that mine mighta if he'da had much of a chance in life.

Henry trying to run with them two left feet he inherited from his mama. The very image wrung a snicker outta me, and a little bit of hurt, too. Lordy, I missed him something fierce, but it was mellowing some, now that I knowed what really killed him.

It was time for me to let him go.

I shoved that thought right outta my head and concentrated on Libby's chatter. Not long after, we pulled into the Millers' empty driveway and got out, me texting Riley an invite to supper that night at the Squirrels'.

The Millers lived in a log cabin-sided double wide set up on what looked like real rock. A fresh-stained, rectangular deck jutted out from the front. Its steps led down to a rock lined pathway mulched in pine straw. A metal mesh table sat to one side of the deck surrounded by four matching chairs. The grass was brown, but well-tended, and small azalea bushes lined the front of the trailer, their roots protected from the cold by a thick layer of pine bark.

Just in case, I poked at the doorbell while Libby went around back and did her thing outta sight of the neighbors and road traffic. The Millers already give us permission to nose around, but it didn't hurt none to let 'em know we was a-starting, though not a peep sounded from inside. Ten to one the entire family was at work or school, this time of day.

I eyed the sun's position in the sky, squinting so as not to hurt my eyes. It was drifting mighty low, which shouldn'ta surprised me a'tall. Libby walked around the side of the trailer on two legs, still fully dressed. Her eyes was wide as saucers and she was shaking her head, flopping the end of her ponytail from one shoulder to t'other.

I hopped down the stairs toward her. "What is it?"

"They took the boy right out of the yard."

That stopped me dead in my tracks. "You're kidding."

"I wish I was. Didn't even need the panther to sniff it out. You can probably smell it, too."

I followed her around back past a fenced in dog yard, minus the dog, and stopped where she told me to.

"Try," she said, so I tested the air with my sniffer and caught that dark smell right about the time Missy's ring went from stone cold to hotter'n fire against my chest.

I yelped and yanked it outta my shirt and off my head, then dangled it by the chain in the air betwixt me and her.

She reached a cautious finger toward it and stopped with an inch between her flesh and the glowing stone. "That's

Missy's magic."

"Her ring," I corrected, though I had no idea if they was one and the same, and weren't rightly interested in the difference right then, if different they was. "It's been lighting up right regular here of late."

"Power likens unto power," she murmured.

Chills run down my spine and I shivered. "Old Mother said the same thing."

"Old Mother?"

"A seer. You ain't met her yet?"

"I don't know everybody," Libby said, her voice kindly droll. She dropped her hand and turned in a slow circle, sniffing ever once in a while as she moved. "I can't believe nobody saw the boy being taken."

"I can't believe the dog didn't bark up a storm."

Libby glanced at the dog yard and wrinkled her nose. "Hmm. It doesn't smell right."

An engine cut off nearby and a car door slammed, killing the questions gathering on my tongue. Libby glanced at me, then I slipped the still hot ring between my shirt and my zipped-up jacket, and we both trotted around the side of the house toward the driveway.

A car with the Clay County, North Carolina, Sheriff's Office logo painted on the side was sitting in the driveway behind a stocky man wearing a police officer's uniform, a stiffly pressed gray shirt tucked into equally pressed black pants over body armor. His hair was bright red and cut snug against his scalp and his pale blue eyes squinted between me and Libby for a minute before his expression cleared and he held out his hand.

"Luke Miller," he said.

I took his hand and measured his grip, not too firm, not too weak. I liked a man what knowed how to shake a woman's hand. "Sunshine Walkingstick. This is my cousin, Libby Squirrel."

A look of pure terror washed over his face, then it was

gone and he held his hand out to Libby. "The Panther Clan is always welcome here."

I cut a glance at Libby and eyed the placid expression her round face was fixed into. Now, that was a plumb interesting way to greet a woman, you ask me. How many folks outside the Eastern Band knowed which clan was what and who belonged to which one?

Don't think I wouldn't be quizzing her about that little tidbit on the way home, especially since she hadn't changed and didn't have the excuse of stuffing her mouth full of a replacement for the calories she'd burned as a painter.

Libby withdrew her hand and tucked it and t'other one into the back pockets of her jeans. "Michael disappeared from the back yard?"

"Mikey," Luke corrected. He held a hand out, pointing us back that way. "Let me show you."

We walked back around the trailer, Libby right to the spot she'd showed me. Luke stopped a coupla feet away and nodded at the place she stood. "Me and him was throwing the ball when my wife called me inside. Light bulb blew. Don't know why she couldn'ta changed it out herself."

Sorrow and a thin thread of anger mingled together in his voice, along with something I couldn't quite put my finger on. Guilt, maybe? I shook it off and said, "What kind of ball?"

"Baseball. The only kind Mikey liked." Luke laughed a little and shook his head, and ran a shaky palm over his mouth. "Wanted to be in the majors, maybe pitch for the Braves one day. God knows, he's got the arm for it."

"That young?" Libby said.

"Oh, yeah. That boy can shoot the ball straight and fast. Man, he's something." The light died outta Luke's eyes and he rubbed his mouth again. "Hard to believe he's gone. I look for him every day when I'm not at work. Check the neighbors, walk the hills. We've had dogs out. The Sheriff wants me to give up. Says I should bury a box and move on. Can you believe it?"

My heart clenched tight in my chest around a well of sorrow and my hands knotted into fists at my side. Oh, I could believe it, just like I could believe Luke still went out looking for his son. I done the same, only I found the critter what got my boy, or thought I had.

No, I corrected myself. I got that critter. It'd just taken a few years for me to get her.

Libby rested a hand on Luke's arm, and when she spoke, her voice was gentle. "We're not going to give up."

He looked at her for a long time. If I hadn't knowed better, I woulda sworn tears glimmered in his eyes. Finally, he nodded and looked away, and Libby's hand slid off his arm and thumped into her side.

I jerked a thumb toward the dog yard. "What kind of dog?"

"Rottweiler. Rotty. That's what Mikey called her." One corner of Luke's mouth turned down. "Rotty was killed in her kennel a couple of days before Mikey went missing. About tore him up, too. He raised her from a pup, him and me both."

Me and Libby exchanged telling glances. Now, that was a mighty big coincidence there.

"You ever figure out what killed her?" I said.

"Maybe a bear or a mountain lion." The last word sorta sputtered outta him. He shot a contrite glance at Libby and muttered a low, "Sorry. Didn't mean nothing by that."

"It wasn't us," Libby said calmly. "I would've heard. Most of us don't roam into residential areas outside our own, if we can help it."

I shook my head. Talk about your open secrets. Lordy, why hadn't I heard about all this before, me being a monster hunter and all?

Luke's mouth opened and closed, and at last, he said, "I wondered if her being killed had anything to do with Mikey. Later, you know? After some of the shock wore off and I logged a few days searching for him."

I floundered around for a minute, searching for a way to say it delicately, then blurted out, "What was her wounds like?"

"Ragged," he said, prompt like. "Clawed up. Her throat first, I reckon. I heard her bark once that night, then nothing. Found her the next morning when I left for work."

Libby sucked in a breath and let it out all at once. "Somebody was watching your home."

"I just wish I could figure out who." Luke raked a hand over his hair, his gaze fixed to the pen. "I haven't been a cop long enough to make that many enemies."

"How long?" I asked.

"Less than a year. I've always wanted to be a cop, then Dad's construction business went belly up. Some asshole from Florida..." He hefted out a sigh and dropped his hand. "Beg pardon. Anyhow, I've been checking out people I've arrested, but they're all clean, far as I can tell."

"You're wasting your time," Libby said bluntly. "This was magic."

"Magic." Luke huffed out a little laugh. "I can't tell my wife that. Natalie, she's a Bible thumping, holy roller. She'll have a cow if I even say that word."

"Then don't tell her it's a witch."

My eyebrows shot up. "A witch?"

"That's what it smells like. Dark magic. Blood." Libby shrugged. "I could be wrong, but I think you're wasting your time on ordinary humans. We're looking for a magic user."

"Magic users ain't all witches," I said. She should know, considering what she was and all.

Libby worked her mouth like she was chewing on something. "But that's what it feels like, doesn't it?"

Since I hadn't ever run up against a witch before, I had not a single, solitary clue what one felt like. It's not that I doubted her. I just didn't know.

We chitchatted for a minute more, then me and Libby

left Luke standing in his back yard, staring into space near the spot where his boy disappeared right out from under his nose.

THE CAR DOOR had barely shut on Libby when she turned to me and said, "Why these kids?"

I cranked the IROC's engine and let it idle while I pondered her question. After a minute or a two, I said, "I don't know."

"Do they look alike or share some specific trait?"

I shook my head, turned the car around, careful not to ding the police car, and eased outta the driveway. "It ain't looks and it ain't age. They's all different shapes and sizes and colors."

Well, not colors. All the young'uns was white, far as I knowed. That didn't rightly mean nothing, what with the sample size being a whopping seven kids. I was thankful it was so small, God's truth, though I was nigh on certain more would turn up, one way or t'other.

"Then what?" Libby asked.

"I don't know."

"You keep saying that."

"Don't know what else to say but the truth."

"God forbid you utter a dishonest word."

A sly bit of sarcasm underscored the words. I ignored it. She could poke at me all she liked, long as she didn't intend no harm, and I reckoned she didn't. Libby had a good heart, she did. Just look at the way she took to me and how she took care of her family and all.

"What's this between Miller and the Panther Clan?" I said.

Libby's expression went hard as granite. "We used to have trouble with some of the local kids teasing our own."

"What happened?"

Her face turned toward me and her chocolate brown eyes took on a hint of green. "We don't have that problem anymore."

I chewed on that for a minute and decided to leave well enough alone, and hoped like aitch ee double hockey sticks that nobody got hurt seriously when the painters decided to protect their own.

The car was a little quieter on the way to her house, over the music playing low on the radio. I don't know what Libby was thinking. My mind was all a-flutter with what she said about the Panther Clan, what she left out, and what we learnt at the Millers'. Whoever them kidnappers was, and it seemed pretty clear there was at least a coupla people involved, judging by what Libby's sniffer turned up, they didn't give two nickels how hard the abducting was. Why, they took poor Mikey right outta his back yard the minute his daddy, a cop, turned his back. What kinda people possessed them sorta nerves?

And killing that dog, too. That pointed to a certain viciousness, not just why it was killed, but the way. Clawed up, Luke said, like an animal, only Libby didn't mention smelling no animal, and she woulda.

The sun slipped fully behind the mountains as we drove and night fell upon us. The minute we turned into Libby's driveway, I tucked all them thoughts away, lest they spill over onto her young'uns. Elijah could take care of himself, what with sharing Libby's painter ways, but the kids? They was still innocent, especially Charlie.

Riley's Range Rover pulled in behind the IROC, before me and Libby even got to the front door. She waved at him, then hustled inside. Children's laughter spilled out the front door when she opened it and was closed off behind her soon as she shut the door.

I tucked my fingers into my pants pockets, warding off the chill, and waited for Riley near the stoop. He slid outta the SUV, grinning like a loon, and trotted toward me, and swooped me into a big ol' bear hug.

"Missed you," he said against my throat.

"Aw, c'mon Riley. You just seen me last night."

"That's a long time to go without loving."

I swatted him on the shoulder, gentle like, and fussed 'til he set me down, then in we went, hand in hand like two lovesick fools.

Which was less than a stone's throw from the truth.

Libby's house was warm and bright and welcoming. Jacob and Wyatt sat on the couch poking at video game controllers. Charlie sat between 'em, one thumb in his mouth, his dark eyes round and serious, like whatever was going on in that video game playing out across the TV screen held the secrets to life and death.

Libby'd slipped away somewhere, likely to freshen up. Elijah shambled outta the kitchen, a dish towel throwed over one shoulder, and grinned at us. He was a big man, tall and solid with a broad face and high cheekbones and silky hair of a dark brown color, worn in a single, long braid down his back. He favored jeans and t-shirts sporting rock and roll bands, most especially ones he'd picked up at the concerts he dragged Libby to along and along.

I sworn, the next time they lit out for one, I was babysitting the boys. It'd been a long time since I had young'uns underfoot, and I was eager to get my hands on 'em for some good old-fashioned fun, games and movies and popcorn and the like. Maybe I'd even let Riley tag along, if he minded his p's and q's.

"You're just in time," Elijah said, his hand held out to Riley.

Riley stepped forward and shook it good, matching the other man grin for grin. "Hey, only a fool would turn down a free meal, and I'm no fool."

"Ain't that the truth," I muttered under my breath.

Right about then, Charlie's gaze turned toward me and he popped off the couch toward me like a cork shooting out of a bottle. I held out my arms and caught him to me, and swung him around for good measure while he giggled and squawked and his older brothers dropped their controllers and begged me to swing them around, too.

Charlie's chubby arms tightened around my neck and his fingers dug into my jacket, holding on for dear life. His little boy smell washed over me, sweat and dirt and baby shampoo all rolled into one, and memory hit, of me holding Henry just like this when he was a little tot.

The parents of them missing kids must be going through hell right now.

My heart squeezed tight in my chest, not because of missing Henry. I just knowed how they felt, is all, knowed exactly how hard it was to abide the loss of a child, and I hated it for 'em. No parent should have to mourn their child, not a single one. Sure, that's the way life turned out ever once in a while. That didn't make it fair nor right, now did it?

Riley took ahold of Charlie and hefted him away from me, high into the air on another one of Charlie's shrieking giggles. I clapped an arm around Jacob and Wyatt each and prodded 'em into chattering about their days in this moment of happiness and family.

THE LIGHTS in the living room was on when I pulled up next to my trailer. I sat there for a minute, surrounded by the low rumble of the IROC's engine, and tapped my forefinger on the steering wheel. I hadn't left the lights on inside, just the porch light, and I knowed it. The two lights was side by side on the wall beside the front door. 'Twas the easiest thing in the world to flip one off and t'other on as I walked out the door.

Weren't Riley in there neither. He left Libby's a good half hour before me and drove straight home. Early morning, he said, right before he promised to come by tomorrow night and kissed me soundly on the lips, right there in front of the entire Squirrel crew.

Not a single other soul shoulda been in my roost other'n

me and him.

Well, nothing for it. I was gonna have to go see who it was.

I shut the engine off, climbed outta the car's warmth into the frost bitten, nighttime air, and fished a tire iron outta the back. Ten to one, Trey or Gentry was in there and I was overreacting, but better safe than sorry. If it weren't one of them, I could always clunk whoever it was over the head and call the police after.

Better, I'd call Fame and let him and the boys deal with my intruder. Word would get out as to what'd happened to the first'un, and I guarantee I'd never have that problem again.

I made it halfway to the door before it opened and Missy stepped onto the porch, light flooding over her like she was the Virgin Mary. I stopped where I was and hollered, "Lord a-mercy, Missy. You about scared the living daylights outta me."

"Sorry, darling. Put the tire iron away and come in. I've made some tea."

The first little worm of worry crept into my gut. Missy outta hearth and home after dark, making tea at this hour of night? Must be something serious.

I pivoted toward the car, popped the tire iron back into its holder, and jogged across the yard and into the trailer. Missy was at the kitchen table, her hands cupped around a steaming mug. A trio of lit candles squatted at the table's center, their flames wavering in the air. I sniffed real good while I shrugged off my jacket and hung it on Riley's hook by the door. Vanilla, lavender, and jasmine, though I weren't so certain about that last'un. My human nose could only separate out so many scents, and that'un weren't as familiar as t'other two was.

I sat down beside her in front of another steaming mug and cupped my own hands around it. No guesses needed there. This late at night the only thing in my cup would be chamomile tea.

"What's up?" I said.

Missy's violet gaze fell to her mug. She stared at it for a minute, twirled it 'round between her palms. Picked it up and sipped once, then clanked its bottom gently against the table's tile mosaic.

Finally, I couldn't take it no more. Hang it all, a woman couldn't sit there all night a-waiting for a body to speak, not when she rose at the rooster's crow ever morning. "You got a bun in the oven?"

Missy sputtered out an indelicate laugh and her eyes went round as saucers. "Where did you get an idea like that?"

"You're just sitting there while your mind spins 'round in circles," I said, fairly blunt. "Just spit it out."

The humor faded from her expression and she glanced away. "Witches."

I took a sip of my tea, waiting for her to elaborate. When she didn't, I prodded. "What about 'em?"

"You know the old tales. Witches kidnapping children." One corner of her pretty mouth turned down and a crease appeared between her delicately arched eyebrows. "Fattening them up and roasting them in an oven."

"Fairytales and superstition."

"Based on a kernel of truth. In the Old World—"

I huffed out a laugh. "You make it sound like it's something ancient."

"In the Old World," she said, kindly firm, "witches abounded, in secret or not. Most were simple healers, wise women knowledgeable in herbs and potions. They harmed no one, though they were blamed for a great deal of ill."

I nodded. That weren't nothing new to me. As little as I knowed about witches, even I had some history under my belt. "What about t'other ones? Not the wise women, but them others."

"True witches versed in magic and spells." Missy's fingers curled into claws against her cup and her fingernails skritched along the painted ceramic. "They exist."

"And which ones is involved here?"

"The latter. Witches, yes, but dark ones. Dark magic. Can't you feel it?"

I studied her for a minute, unsure which part of that to comment on, and finally settled on, "I can smell the red magic, when it's strong."

Missy shuddered. "Red magic. So apropos. That's blood magic, Sunny, deep and dark and dreadful. It's death magic."

"Death magic?"

"Magic wrought by the cessation of life, particularly human life."

I hadn't needed an explanation, just a confirmation, but I took what she give me and filed it away along with the rest of what I was learning. Witches, real witches, practicing an awful sort of spell. "Why?"

"Power. Longevity." She shuddered again and her fingers twitched against the cup. "For the love of death, the cruelty of it. Why does anyone deal in death?"

Now, that was the best question I'd heard in a while. Didn't have an answer for her, though. "Why are you telling me all this?"

"Because I think you have a witch problem on your hands."

"Witches kidnapping children, you mean? Using 'em in some kind of dark ceremony?"

"Yes."

"And you know this how?"

Her gaze dropped to her mug. She brought it to her mouth, sipped a bare drop of liquid, set the cup down. "I put out some feelers."

"What kind?"

"The kind accumulated over a lifetime."

"Any of them feelers magical in nature?"

That give her pause. "A few," she said slowly.

"And you?"

Her lips pressed together and her thumb went a-tapping

70

against the mug.

I waited her out, just sat there sipping my own tea, and stared at her, not outta rudeness, but outta curiosity. I'd knowed Missy a long time, long enough to know her heart and her mind. Not long enough to know her past, and apparently not long enough to know all the intricate details of her making. Missy had secrets. I don't know why that'd never occurred to me before that very moment.

She took a final sip of her tea, then stood and carried her cup to the sink. "I don't know what you're talking about."

I stood and followed her and leaned a hip against the counter beside her. "Don't lie to me, Missy. Libby can smell your magic."

She placed her cup in the sink, turned to me, and placed her hands on my cheeks, and her gaze bore into mine, violet to brown, bore into me and through me, seeing ever thing I was, ever thing I could be, and ever thing I'da never in a million years thought on being. "Fame's expecting me. Goodnight, darling. Sleep well."

Missy's hands slid off my cheeks, then she turned and walked across the kitchen into the living room and out the door, her booted feet a bare whisper against the shag carpet.

I stood where she left me, my mind whirling 'round and 'round like a thousand birds flying at cross purposes. Against my chest, the ring hummed and glowed, casting a dim, red light into the air around me.

9

The next morning, I woke with the clear, bright certainty on what I needed to do that day, after a night spent tossing and turning and chewing over that odd conversation with Missy.

Something was going on with her, something dangerous and dark, something she shoulda told us a long, long time ago, but what? What'd she got herself into, or what was it she come from that made her so skeered she couldn't trust me with it? Them questions hummed in my bones, lighting my blood on fire and nigh on torturing my brain.

Hang it all, a body could only take so many mysteries before they plumb wore her out.

I fried up some fatback and taters for breakfast whilst making a list of corners I could pry into on my way to figuring out how to track down witches. Was there a local coven or what? I shook my head and jotted down a note to pick up a reference book covering the subject, seeing as how not a one of mine dealt with 'em in any depth.

Well, not beyond the odd fable or two. I had them a-plenty, but I had a sneaky suspicion I wouldn't find what I needed in *Grimm's Fairy Tales.*

It being Saturday and all, if I wanted to suss out another book, I needed to shake a leg, seeing as how the public library in Clayton closed at noon.

Right as I was sitting down at the kitchen table in front of a plate of breakfast, notebook and coffee to the side, a firm knock hit my front door. I glanced down at the steaming pile of fried taters covered in cornmeal gravy and sighed. Dadgummit. I shoulda knowed better'n to fix a fancy breakfast on a day when work beckoned.

Resigned, I hollered, "Come on in."

The door opened and in walked Sheriff Treadwell, carrying the cold and a stack of folders in with him. He was wearing thick carpenter jeans and a flannel shirt under his unbuttoned canvas jacket. A worn baseball cap emblazoned with the sheriff's department logo covered his graying hair and scuffed brown boots peeked out beneath the jeans' lower hems.

He shut the door behind himself and said, "Morning, Sunshine. You got a minute?"

You know that scene in that movie, whatsit? The one about the little boy wanting that bb gun? Anyhow, in that movie, one of his friends touched his tongue to a frozen flagpole on a dare and got it stuck there so good, they had to call the authorities in to pry him loose.

That's what I felt like right then, like my hind end was froze firm to my seat and my fingers to the silverware they was wrapped around. I musta looked like a deer caught in headlights or something. That's how shocked I was by my early morning visitor.

Finally, sense knocked me upside the head and I set my fork down on my plate and stood. "Morning, Sheriff. What brings you to my neck of the woods?"

He held up them folders and waggled 'em at me. "Got some files for you to look over. Sorry it took me so long. Some of the nearby police departments were a little slow to respond."

"I appreciate the help," I said, and I did. Lord knows, I hadn't expected him to walk a single step outta his way to aid me, missing young'uns or no. "You want some breakfast or coffee or something?"

He eyed my plate real good and got an odd look on his face. "That your mama's cornmeal gravy recipe?"

"Yessir, it sure is."

"Then I'll have some, if you've got any to spare."

I bit back my second surprise of the day and hustled to throw a plate together for him. "If you're gonna sit and eat, might as well be comfortable."

A faint smile creased his mouth, and he set the files down, shrugged off his coat, and hung it and his cap up on the hooks by the door. "Riley says he comes by regularly."

I eyed the sheriff over my shoulder, and yup, I admit it. I struggled with being civil for a bit. In the end, I took the high road. This man was Riley's daddy, after all. Least I could do was try for polite.

"He does. Me and him is dating."

"So he says."

Not a hint of censure tinged his words, so I held up the plate full of taters and gravy and said, "Fatback and biscuits?"

"I'd love some, thanks."

I dished him up some, set the plate down across the table from me, then backtracked to the coffee pot and poured him a mug full. We sat there for a while in near silence, tucking into our breakfast. It was like sitting across the table from an older version of Riley. They held their forks the same, sat up at the table the same, even sipped their coffee the same way. I sworn, if I closed my eyes, they'd probably sound the same, too.

Though I weren't tempted a bit to do so. Best to keep

both eyes and ears open when the law plopped down at your kitchen table. Never mind that I ain't never caused not a lick of trouble in my life, outside of giving birth to Henry without the benefit of a ring on my finger. Weren't long ago when this man arrested my uncle for murder, knowing full well he weren't guilty.

I was a forgiving woman, in my own way, but I dang sure weren't gonna forget a sin like that.

About halfway through cleaning his plate, Sheriff Treadwell glanced up at me. "I thought about dating your mama once."

I near about choked on a sip of coffee. Real polite like, I swallowed it down and patted my mouth dry with my paper napkin. Lord a-mercy, what was he thinking, dumping something like that on me in the middle of eating?

"We met at a football game," he continued, like he hadn't noticed me a-sputtering. "No, after the game. I was a running back for Habersham back then."

Habersham being the next county south of Rabun, one of the local public high school's biggest rivals back in the day. "Fame was the quarterback about that time, weren't he?"

The sheriff's grin held a little mischief and mean rolled into his humor. "He was."

I grunted and forked taters into my mouth, hoping to bottle up my retort.

He chuckled and sipped at his coffee, and the skin around his eyes crinkled up. "One night after we played up here, a bunch of us laid in wait outside the locker room, hoping to start something. Well, you know how boys are. We were always looking to start something, especially after nearly getting our tails handed to us by a scrawny bunch of white boys. Fame had an arm back then. Did he tell you he got offered an athletic scholarship at Georgia Tech?"

"I knowed he went to Tech for a while," I said, feeling out the words like they was treading through shark infested waters. "Didn't know nothing about no scholarship."

"Oh, he had them in plenty."

I let that roll around in my head for a minute, and finally said, "So y'all laid in wait hoping to stir something up."

"It was homecoming, I think. There was a big dance, and some of our kids had been invited. You know how it is. Nobody wants to date the people they go to school with." He shook his head and evened gravy out over the rest of his taters. "Anyway, we were hanging out near the home team's locker room, trying to be casual and failing miserably, and up comes this spitfire of a girl. She had the prettiest eyes back then."

Back before she killed my daddy.

He didn't say the words, but I could about hear 'em, and danged if they didn't quash what was left of my appetite. I set my fork down and picked up my coffee cup, waiting for him to continue.

"Marched right up to me," he said, "and stuck her finger in my chest. She was maybe a foot and a half shorter than me, but man, she was pretty. I knew who she was right off. The Carsons all have that look to them."

"And Carsons and Treadwells don't never mix," I popped off, somewhat bitter.

Chip's gaze sharpened on me right then. His mouth firmed up and he nodded once. "Bad blood. An old family feud. But your mama was something. Enough to tempt me, anyway, so I stood there and let her lecture me, then I asked her if she was going with anyone to the dance. She stuck her fists on her hips and looked me up and down and said, 'I'm only thirteen, you perv.'"

I snorted out a laugh, nearly snorting coffee along with it. "Yeah, that sounds like Mama, all right."

He shook his head, and danged if a reluctant smile didn't tilt his mouth. "She was something," he repeated. "Shooed us off before we could do any damage. I followed her into the dance, lied my ass off to get in, too, just so I could hang out with her a little while. Fame came in hand in hand with Ann. I took one look at her and forgot all about your mama."

"True love?" I said, only half sarcastic.

"For me, anyway. She was all tangled up in Fame. Wouldn't give me the time of day back then, and didn't until—" His gaze dropped to his plate and he sat back in his chair. "Later, after your daddy died, Ann talked me into letting your mama come over and cook for the inmates. That was before she was convicted, back when the old jail under the courthouse was still in use."

"And you let her?"

"Ann trusted her, and she loved you. I think she would've done anything for you."

"Mama?"

"Ann, but your mama, too. Have you visited her lately?"

"Back around Christmas. Why?"

He shook his head and sighed and set his fork down, then draped his hands along the edge of the table, one to either side of his plate. "I know you think I target your family, Sunny, and sometimes I do. Ann jumped all over me for arresting Fame last year, and she should've. I knew he wasn't guilty. Hell, we all know what his wife was like."

I clamped my mouth shut and vowed not to utter a single harsh word about Lily, her nor Ferd neither one. Let the dead sleep in peace, far as I was concerned. Less trouble that way for ever body concerned.

"And all those other campers getting torn up," he continued. "Thank God you figured out what it was and tracked it down."

"That's what I do."

"I know. We all do." He scrubbed both hands over his face, and when he dropped 'em in his lap, he looked tired, worn to the bone even, like the weight of the world rested on his shoulders. "I've been chipping away at a mystery for a long time, Sunny, and I think it's one you can help me solve."

I tapped a finger against my coffee cup, mimicking Missy without meaning to. "Your brother went missing."

His gaze sharpened on me again, then he huffed out a laugh and shook his head. "Yeah, something like that."

"You blame yourself." I sipped my coffee, grimaced at the cold liquid washing over my tongue, and stood. "I don't think you should."

"Why's that?"

I snagged his coffee cup, took it and mine to the sink and dumped 'em out. Filled 'em back up with fresh, give his to him, and sat back down again. "Can I trust you?"

For a minute, he looked like I'd mortally offended him. I stared at him, my gaze steady as a rock, and gradually, he faded back into that worn out look. "If anyone else had asked me that, I'd have taken him outside and beat the ever-loving hell out of him."

"But not me."

"No, not you. You of all people have reason to question my integrity." He scooted back his chair, abrupt like, and stood, then snagged the files he'd left laying on the couch and brung 'em to the table. "You read these, and when you're finished, you decide if you can trust me."

I grabbed the files and slid 'em carefully across the mosaic-topped table. "Fair enough."

"In the meantime, I've got a tip for you. An anonymous tip," he said, before I could poke and pry. He riffled through the folders from where he sat and pulled out a single sheet of paper stuck between two. "Anonymous source, as far as you're concerned. Just an address, but I was assured this was where you needed to start."

I studied the paper and the handwritten address scrawled across it, and frowned. "I ain't rightly familiar with Atlanta."

"Google Maps," he suggested. "If you need backup, you call me and I'll drive down there with you. I don't want you putting yourself at risk the way you did last December."

I glanced up at him, and my frown turned into a scowl. "I can take care of myself. Been doing it for a long time now."

"And you've been beaten black and blue a few times too

many for my son's peace of mind," he said, blunt as a sledgehammer. "Take me or him, but take somebody."

"I'll think about it." And that's the best promise I could make him. "You want me to box you up them leftovers to take with you? I made too much. Reckon I'm getting a little too used to cooking for two, what with Riley and all."

He glanced down at his plate and his expression cleared. "I'd like that, if it's no trouble."

"None a'tall," I said, and that was the plain truth. "I appreciate you bringing this by. It was mighty kind of you."

"It's the least I could do."

For the missing young'uns or his missing brother?

I bit back the question and tucked the leftovers into a plastic container. He pulled his coat on and stood in front of the door, fingering the brim of his cap, watching me like I was some rare species of bug he didn't know what to do with. Finally, I handed over the container and tucked my hands in the back pockets of my jeans, where they couldn't do nothing stupid like open the door and shove him outta it.

"Thank you, Sunny," he said, then he raised his hand and, real hesitant, brushed it across my shoulder.

I seen him out, shut the door behind him, and leaned my backside against the cold metal. Well, if that didn't beat all. I'd have to tell Riley all about his daddy's little visit when I seen him later, but for dang sure, I weren't gonna breathe word one to Fame. Last thing I needed was for him to get all riled up and get that blood feud a-going all over again, just when I was enjoying the détente.

THEM FILES snared my attention soon as I got the breakfast dishes cleaned up, pretty much shooing off any intention I had of going to the library and hunting down them witches. Well, references to witches anyhow. 'Til the good sheriff give me that address, I hadn't a clue how to track 'em down.

I snorted. Anonymous tip my hiney. Ten to one, was

Missy what give it to him.

The missing kids was organized by county, and within each county, by jurisdiction, if they went missing inside some city's limits. I started with Rabun County, since it was the thickest file by far, and flipped through the paperclipped pages, one page per young'un. County records come first and it had the most pages. No surprise there. They was a few incorporated towns scattered throughout the county, aside from the county seat of Clayton, but only a few city police departments.

I sat back and tallied the total in my head, not counting any of the communities without any law a'tall. There was Clayton, of course, since it was the county seat, then Mountain City and Dillard to the north and Tallulah Falls along the southern border shared with Habersham County.

No, that weren't quite right. I wrinkled my nose up and counted again, and remembered Sky Valley, up the mountain east of Dillard, along the North Carolina line. But they probably hadn't had a kid go missing, seeing as how mostly retired folk lived up there, far as I knowed.

I flipped through the clipped papers again, and sure enough, not a single stack was from Sky Valley.

T'others had a few, though, but 'twas the ones missing from the county I was interested in, since more'n likely the cities had handed them over to the county and its larger number of resources. I pulled that stack out, set the folder on my desk, and spread the papers across the kitchen table, letting 'em overlap when the table got too full. Some of the pages included pictures, some didn't. Some was typed, quite a few was hand-written. I run a finger across the papers, skimming the information, and got my third surprise of the morning.

Or was it my fourth?

I'd lost count, that's for sure, but I let it go and propped my hands on my hips, gazing down at the paper-covered table as my mind twisted and whirled.

The sheriff brung me decades worth of missing kids files. Summaries, sure, but enough information to hint at a pattern. I scanned the dates again and tallied 'em up, best I could, then I pulled out the city files and spread 'em out along with the county's, lining up dates.

There was a pattern here. Not a regular pattern, no. A forty-year gap here, a twenty-five-year gap there, but sure enough, there was a cycle of two or three kids disappearing within a few months of each other ever few decades or so. If I could just figure it out...

Determined now, I pulled out t'other counties and, heedless of origin, sorted ever thing by date, and when I was done, I stepped back again and stared in growing horror at what emerged.

Somebody'd been kidnapping kids in this area for decades, maybe longer even. I tapped a finger against one page, a photocopy of barely legible newspaper clippings and handwritten letters interspersed with Sheriff Treadwell's bold scrawl, and zeroed in on a single year.

1863.

At the height of Lincoln's War, somebody stole kids away from their mamas' bosoms, stole 'em away and done...what?

Missy's words drifted to me, *dark magic, blood magic*, and a chill run down my spine, like somebody walked over my grave. Was they really witches out there, gathering up kids for some unnamed evil? What kind of ceremony was they performing, and why? Longevity, as Missy suggested, but of what sort?

Witches looking to extend their lives maybe, or—?

A thought struck me dead center and I inhaled sharp like. Not witches. A whole gaggle of witches tromping through the countryside woulda been noticed back in the nineteenth century, when communities was tight knit, but a coupla strangers, or maybe just one?

One or two wouldn'ta raised much fuss a'tall, if they

worked it right.

I stared down at the papers for a long while, letting my mind gnaw on the problem, then I gathered the papers together, sorted 'em back into their proper piles, and pulled out a pack of different colored highlighters and my case notebook. Sheriff Treadwell musta put in years of work tracking down some of this stuff (*decades*, something inside me whispered). The least I could do was use it well and wise, to the benefit of the young'uns what was missing now.

RILEY COME IN while I was still bent over the table, reading the files his daddy brung me. He shed his coat and hat, hung 'em up by the door, and flopped onto the edge of the couch. "What's that?"

"Missing kids." I leaned back and stretched and felt ever bone in my spine crack and pop. Lordy, had I been sitting there that long? "Time is it?"

"Around one. I'm running late."

I waved that off and propped my elbows on the table and my chin in my hands. "I thought you was working all day?"

He shook that fire-topped head of his and bent over his boots, his fingers swift along the laces. "Just half a day today. It's too cold out for spotlighting and nobody in his right mind wants to wade into water and fish."

I snickered, even as an image of Harley Jimpson popped into my head. That old coot'd have his grand young'uns out there no matter how cold it was, if he thought he could pull one over on somebody. Especially a gov'ment somebody.

I pushed my chair back and stood up. "What you want for lunch? I got sandwich makings."

"The way I hear it, you've got more than that." He toed his boots off, set 'em by the door, and ambled over to me, his hazel eyes full of mischief. "In fact, you've been holding out on me. Cornmeal gravy?"

"You been talking to your daddy."

"He called on his way home, after he dropped by here." Riley settled in front of me and cupped my hips with his paws. "Mom wants us come over and have lunch with them after church tomorrow."

My eyes about rolled outta my head. "I ain't breaking bread with your daddy."

"You already have."

I hated it when he was all reasonable and logical and such like, so I did what come natural. I dug in my heels and scowled up at him. "I got work to do. If you ain't noticed, there's a passel of young'uns missing and they ain't gonna get found if I sit around jawing the fat with the sheriff."

"Sunny, baby." Riley's voice was low and so soothing, I relaxed in spite of my mad. He bumped my hips into his and curled his arms around me, pulling me in close to his chest. "He took the first step. Maybe you could try meeting him in the middle."

Well, when he put it like that.

I closed my eyes and turned my face into his chest. His hands was chilled against my back, but here over his heart, he was toasty warm and smelled of sawdust and winter air. "I reckon I could try, but only 'cause you asked nice."

He chuckled, vibrating my cheek where it rested against his work shirt. "That's my gal. Need some help with that?"

I shook my head, eyes still closed, and let my hands creep around his waist. "I've about got it. Lots of parents needing a visit, but right now, I gotta track down a coven of witches."

"Seriously?"

"Yup. Missy warned me about 'em—"

"How did Missy know?"

Now that was the question, weren't it? "No idea, but then your daddy showed up with an address I'm supposed to check out."

"My dad," Riley said slowly, "gave you an address for witches."

"Anonymous tip."

"Right. Like I believe that."

"I didn't neither." We fell quiet for a minute, then something I'd been thinking on all morning spilled outta my mouth. "Maybe that ain't their only address."

"Come again?"

"That Atlanta place. That's a far piece from here, a coupla hours at least."

"So why travel that far to kidnap kids, if they're behind it at all?"

Trust Riley to hit the nail on the head. "Exactly. Seems like a long way to go, even if a body didn't want to fish in their own pond, so to speak."

"If they really are witches, wouldn't they need a place for ceremonies or..." He sighed, then tightened his arms around me. "I don't know much about witches, but it seems strange for them to be located in the city. I mean, aren't they into nature and all that?"

"Wiccans," I murmured. "Pagans."

"What's the difference?"

"No idea." But I intended to find out. Later, after we finished cuddling.

"Maybe I should call Belinda," Riley said.

That got my attention. My eyes popped open and I leaned back and glared at him. "Why you wanna call that she-devil for?"

"She's a real estate agent. She has connections. If we can figure out who these witches are, maybe we can track down any land they own through Belinda."

I was already shaking my head and backing away from him. "No way in aitch ee double hockey sticks do I want that hussy involved in this." Even if her niece's young'un was missing. "She ain't nothing but trouble, and let me tell you, Riley Treadwell. If I catch you within spitting distance of her, there'll be trouble the likes of which you ain't never seen before."

A slow smile spread across his face and danged if he didn't cross his arms over his chest and grin down at me. "Jealous?"

I sputtered my indignation out and hooked my hands on my hips. "What've I got to be jealous for?"

"Oh, I don't know. The fact that she's my friend."

I weren't gonna stand there and listen to that nonsense. I pivoted around on a socked foot and marched into the bedroom.

And didn't get three feet when Riley's arms come around me from behind and lifted me plumb off the shag carpet.

"Whoa there, Nelly," he said, laughter so thick in his voice, I couldn't hardly understand him. "Don't go rushing off just when it's getting good."

I kicked back and bucked in his arms. "Let me go, Riley, or so help me—"

"So help you what?" He set me down and pressed his body against mine, trapping me between him and the kitchen counter, and danged if his erection didn't push into my back through our clothes. "Am I your feller or what?"

Already, a haze of desire was befuddling my head. I crossed my arms together and leaned my forearms against the counter, wiggling my butt into him without even meaning to. "You're my feller."

"Then what've you got to be jealous of?" His hands slid down my sides and back up again, and he leaned close and whispered in my ear. "I've been fantasizing about taking you just like this."

My eyelids slid shut as heat shuddered through me, and danged if I didn't forget all about that nasty worm Belinda Arrowood for the rest of the afternoon.

10

Later, Riley talked me into letting him tag along while I met parents that afternoon. I hated showing up on folks' stoops out of the blue like that, but what else could I do? A deep uneasiness rested low in my gut, right alongside urgency. I needed to be out there doing something, anything to find them kids. I weren't picky what it was neither, long as it took me one step closer to tracking 'em down.

Sure, I could wait 'til Monday and hunt for them families through Facebook and whatnot, or even use Riley's computer that night to do the same, but why wait? Little Sophie been missing for days and days. Weren't one blessed soul no closer to finding her now than they was when she wandered off into the woods, or was carried there.

And that's what worried me. The thought of what mighta whisked them young'uns off, and what they might be doing to 'em, skeered the ever-loving bejesus outta me.

We managed to visit three families in southwestern

North Carolina before dark set in good, and all three of 'em was the same. Working class folks, some barely making ends meet. Their kids disappeared right outta their own yards. The police done give up.

Ever time I heard that story, my heart tightened in my chest, a little more and a little more 'til by nightfall, it felt like a hand was wrapped around it, squeezing hard.

I was floundering like a fish outta water, stumbling around trying to piece together mysteries other folks couldn't solve. What good was I to anybody like that? What could I do to help them young'uns? Or was there any way of tracking 'em down a'tall?

Riley drove me across the mountain from Murphy into Franklin and fed me supper, then coaxed me into a late movie. I sat there watching glamorous folk flit across the big screen, my mind reduced to a turmoil of what ifs and maybes.

Halfway through, Riley eased his arm around my shoulders and bent his head close to mine. "You'll figure it out," he whispered. "I know you can. Maybe Dad can help."

I recoiled instinctively away from the suggestion (A Carson asking a Treadwell for help? Never!), even as a tiny corner of my mind grabbed ahold of that idea and refused to let go. Was it time for me to bring in the big guns? Or should I keep floundering around on my own?

I didn't know and I sure weren't gonna ponder it no more that night. I tucked as much of my worries away as I could and focused on the movie, letting it and Riley soothe me for a good long while.

RILEY DRUG ME to church the next morning, and I followed along meek as a lamb to slaughter, wearing the Sunday-go-to-meetings dress I wore to Henry's memorial service some time back. It felt wrong sitting there on the cushioned pew squeezed between him and his mama, what with him having woke me to some good ol' fashioned loving before he hurried me into the shower to get ready.

Though if God wanted only the sinless in church, he was bound to get a passel of empty pews come Sunday morn.

So I rose and sat with the rest of the congregation, sang in a half-hearted warble thankfully drowned out by Riley's solid baritone, and let him carry me to his mama and daddy's house for a lunch I was sure'd be about as comfortable as sitting on a porcupine.

Ann had left a beef stew simmering in the crockpot and paired it with rolls and coleslaw she whipped up the night before. She sat me down between her and Chip on each end and across from Riley at the rectangular table in their formal dining room. A fancy damask tablecloth covered the wood, draping elegantly against my thighs, and a fresh flower centerpiece sat squat in the middle between two red candles twisted into silver candlesticks. The china was bone thin and decorated with tiny violets under a circle of gold, entirely too fine for the hearty Southern meal Ann had prepared.

I folded my hands in my lap, careful to keep 'em well away from the bowl resting on the plate in front of me. Thank the good Lord Ann'd kept the silverware to the bare minimum, else I was liable to get all tangled up in the fanciness and make a dadblamed fool of myself.

The three of 'em made polite conversation around me. I took tiny, timid bites of the stew Riley'd ladled out for me, even as he crumbled a quarter pone of cornbread into his and spooned it up like he hadn't eat in a week.

Which I knowed dadgum well he had, since I fed him myself.

During a small lull in the talking, Ann turned to me and said, "Chip told me Henry's half-sister has gone missing."

I near about dropped my spoon into my bowl. "Yes'm, her and a few other young'uns."

Ann hummed a little under her breath and set her own spoon tidily to one side of her plate. "I do hope you find her."

Me, too. I squeezed my eyes shut against the pang in my

heart and blurted out, "She's got a brother, a little chunk of a baby with Dumbo ears and a sweet smile. They named him Terrence Henry after his big brother."

Riley's spoon clattered into his bowl, and my eyes popped open to the downturn of his mouth and heat in his eyes. Ann reached across the table and clasped her hand on my wrist, drawing my attention to the sad smile gracing her own mouth.

"That was sweet of them, to remember our Henry that way."

"Yes'm, it—" A frog the size of a boulder lodged itself in my throat, choking off my words, and I shook my head, hoping she understood my agreement. It'd been downright sweet, and I did appreciate it, but Lordy, did I miss my baby boy right then.

Chip wiped his mouth with a cloth napkin, folded it, and set it beside his plate, his eyes downcast. "I'm going to Atlanta first thing in the morning."

A funny kinda tingling snaked up my spine, and without asking, I knowed exactly what he was gonna do once he got down there. My eyes met Riley's across the centerpiece of hothouse roses and lilies, and it come to me then like a jolt of lightning on a sunny day, right outta the blue.

I weren't gonna be able to find them kids on my own. If I wanted to do 'em justice, and I did with all my bitty heart, then I was gonna have to break down and ask for help, ask for it, beg for it, grovel if I had to.

For a minute, I struggled against the knowledge, torn between needing help and trusting somebody else enough to receive it. I been on my own too long, been abandoned and taken for granted, and had the trust ground outta me by too many folks for relying on somebody else to come natural.

Then there was Riley, staring back at me, his hazel eyes glimmering, and of a sudden, the day we met popped into my head. Him in the lake playing with his friends. That snake gliding through the water. Me snatching it out and breaking its back without thinking twice on it.

And a sudden realization hit me, jolting through me about as hard as t'other one had. That day set the pattern of my life, not Mama killing Daddy when he run off with that vacuum cleaner salesman, not Terry leaving me high and dry with a young'un on the way, not Henry's death at the hands of my grandmother, but the day I snatched that snake outta the water. That was the day I took on the monsters of the world. That was the day I become who I was meant to be, and it was the day I stepped forward into the world on my own.

That day, I learnt I could do near about anything, no help needed. It'd set a bad precedent, and me in my stubbornness, I'd let it.

And here I was now faced with the possibility that them young'uns might still be alive, on the cusp of knowing I couldn't save 'em on my own, with help just an arm's length away from me to my left and across from me and to my right.

I'd be a fool not to take it when the life of my boy's half-sister was at stake.

I twisted my arm outta Ann's gentle grasp, then took her hand while I looked her husband square in the face, him what'd caused enough trouble for my family to last a lifetime and a half. "I'd like to go with you, if you don't mind me tagging along."

Chip's gaze rose to mine, slow as molasses in the cold, and finally he said, "I'd like that."

Riley grinned at me across the table and Ann's hand tightened against mine, and some of the uneasiness drained away, and with it some of the doubts. I was doing the right thing, accepting aid from Riley's daddy. I just knowed I was.

Now, if I could only find a way to tell Fame I was making hay with his mortal enemy, I figured I'd about have it made.

11

Since me and the good sheriff was leaving for Atlanta from Clayton bright and early the next day, I spent the night at Riley's. I been there before, of course. Me and him been dating long enough for me to be familiar with the layout. I just hadn't stayed over since we started doing the down and dirty.

Turns out, the before and after of throwing sex into the mix was nigh on the same. We went straight from his folks' house to Persimmon so I could pack an overnight bag, then we swung by the grocery store on the way to his place and picked up stuff for chili. It was game day, basketball or something, and that's what he wanted to eat. He even promised to cook it if I'd sit beside him during the game.

I was fine doing that, but the best part of it was, he settled me in beside him with his laptop. I reckoned he was getting to know me a mite too well, but for once, I didn't mind not one bit. He watched the game with one hand curled around my toes, where I was sitting cross legged, and the other holding a beer, in between random trips to the kitchen to check on the chili. Ever once in a while, he'd grunt at a play and I'd look up from snooping through Facebook to see what was a-going on, and that's how we spent the evening.

It was nice, being with him like that, and it was nice having easy access to the Internet and social media. I learned lots about the families of the missing young'uns before we ate supper.

When our bellies started growling louder than whatever was happening on the TV, Riley dished us up two big ol' bowls of his homemade chili and we ate right there on his couch, like normal Americans for a change.

A coupla bites in, he said, "You try searching for those witches online?"

I stopped chewing the chili in my mouth for a second, the question poked me so hard. Dang it all, I hadn't even thought to. Good thing I had him along to jog my memory. I finished chewing real quick like and swallowed even quicker, and managed not to choke myself in my hurry. "Will after supper."

"Belinda suggested—"

My spoon clattered into my bowl. "What'd I tell you about her?"

He grinned real big and kept his eyes on the cornbread he was stirring into his chili. "*Someone* suggested we do a search for the address and see what comes up."

"Pfft."

"I bet you can find out all sort of interesting things just by that one search."

I cut my eyes at him, shook my head, and finally let it go. He was right, for one, and for another, I weren't gonna poke at him when the evening was going so well. Even I weren't that mean. Still, I weren't so forgiving I was gonna let him off the hook without making him squirm a mite first. "You can help, since you got time on your hands."

"What time? I'm watching the game."

"The way I figure it," I said, sweet as honey, "if you got time to talk to another woman, you sure enough got time to help this'un."

He laughed so hard, I thought he was gonna spill his chili. "God, Sunny. You're the best."

I hadn't a clue how I went from passive-aggressive to being the best in the same sentence, but if that's what he wanted to think of me, who was I to tell him different?

Sure enough, a simple search turned up all sorts of stuff. The address turned out to be in an office building located smack dab in the middle of Buckhead. Riley showed me how to turn the street map into a satellite view, then he did something so we got a 3D view of the surrounding area. It was almost like standing on the street, only without the noise and fumes of traffic and city folk.

A coupla other things popped up along with the address, the first being the name of a business there. The Goddess Within. Hunh. Appeared to be some kinda herbal beauty store and spa or something. Not the sorta place I'da touched in a million years, 'less somebody give it to me.

The second thing what turned up was names, and not just the owners but neighbors and associates and so much other stuff, my head went a little dizzy.

I wrote ever thing down, dutiful as ever in my search, then backtracked and checked to see if the business had a website, and it did. I clicked through to the about page and scanned it, and found a coupla pictures of folks supposedly working there.

Funny thing. They was all women, and some of 'em matched the cornucopia of names what'd popped up in the associates list.

Something caught my eye, the mention of a nature camp in north Georgia.

A funny tingle run down my spine. Ever so slow, I pointed the mouse at the link and clicked. Up popped another page containing a brightly worded description dancing on the page around a picture of a simply constructed lodge set against the mountains.

My gut tightened and a voice whispered in my head, stirring instinct.

There.

I checked the address listed on the bottom of the page and was completely unsurprised at the mailing address. Helen, just a coupla counties over. So close, so close.

That something inside me stirred again, jarring me outta the daze the picture put me in. I startled, as if coming awake, and wrote the camp's address down, then drew stars around it, over and over again, stars and moons and symbols I never seen before, and Missy's ring burned bright against my skin, bright and hot and so red, the glow filled me up.

Riley's hand come down on mine, startling me, and the pencil's point snapped off. "What're you doing, baby?"

I glanced down at his hand holding mine, at the pointless pencil and the white knuckled grip I had on it, and at the symbols, dozens of symbols I didn't even remember drawing, and I swallowed hard. "I don't know."

He brung my hand up, pried the pencil out real gentle like, and kissed my fingertips one by one. "Maybe you should take a break," he said, just as gentle.

I shook my head, flexed the stiff outta my fingers. "I'm ok. You just..."

"I just what?"

"Maybe take that page and put it away for a bit, just 'til I finish up."

He stared at me for a minute, then he stroked a hand over my stick straight hair. "Sure, baby. I can do that."

He tore the page outta my notebook and put it in the bedroom, outta sight, and I gradually settled down and spent the rest of the evening searching out ever thing I could on each and ever one of them women, news and images and, shoot, even birthdays and political affiliations. Ever thing went into a handy dandy Word document Riley set up for me. He made me stop around 9:30, and good thing, too, as my hands was like claws, I been typing so long, and my legs was going numb from sitting still. He give me his daddy's email address and I sent what I found, including that special little camp, along to the sheriff while Riley texted his dad and let him know it was on the way.

After I was done, we brushed our teeth and fell into bed together, and I took ever bit of my happiness at finding something out about them witches out on him, to his ever-loving pleasure.

But that paper, the one I doodled all them foreign signs on, it stayed locked away, safe outta my reach, though it haunted my dreams all the night long.

SHERIFF TREADWELL knocked on Riley's door about the same time I pulled on my clothes after a hot shower. Riley was still in bed, his head half buried under his pillow, and the windows in his bedroom was barely lit by the breaking dawn.

I scurried to the door and let the sheriff in, and grunted a hello as I shut the door behind him. "Gotta get my boots on. You want some coffee?"

He shook his head and run a cold-reddened palm over his mouth. "Figured we'd stop at McDonald's on the way out of town."

If we was back home, I'da invited him in to sit a spell while I finished getting dressed, but we wasn't at the trailer and I didn't wanna overstep my own welcome in Riley's apartment. I nodded and hurried back into the bedroom, shoved my socked feet into my boots and tied 'em real quick, then bussed Riley's cheek and left him laying there.

The sheriff was standing exactly where I left him, his fingers tucked into the front pockets of worn jeans under a sturdy canvas jacket, his gaze glued to the living room windows where the sun was barely warming the day. Dark circles marred the skin under his eyes, which had sagged into early morning bags I suspected was put there by too much work and not enough sleep more'n age.

His mouth opened like he was gonna say something, then his teeth snapped together and he run a weather roughened hand over his beardless chin.

I raised my eyebrows at him. "Go ahead. Spit it out."

He looked at me for a minute, them eyes of his nearly boring holes through me, they was so wicked sharp. "That camp you mentioned in your email."

Stars and moons and strange symbols danced in my head, and for a minute, the ring burned bright and hot under my shirt.

"What about it?" I said slowly.

"What did you make of it?"

I shrugged my jacket on, zipped it up, and tried not to get lost in the lure of ancient magic spinning through my head. "It's mighty close to where them kids disappeared."

"Not too close, though," he murmured, almost like he was speaking to himself.

"Not too close," I agreed. "But close enough to drive."

Or maybe something else. I poked and prodded my memory and finally pulled up Libby telling me about how them scents she picked up what'd just disappeared. Was magical teleportation even a thing? What else would explain them kids vanishing into thin air?

"What does your gut say?"

My eyes snapped around to his. "Why d'you ask?"

He shrugged his broad shoulders under his jacket and shifted his stance from one booted foot to t'other. "Just humor me."

Well, if he insisted. "That's where we need to be," I said, blunt as a sledgehammer on concrete.

He nodded slowly. "Ok."

"Ok what?"

"That's where we'll go."

It woulda shocked me less if he'da pulled out his concealed carry and shot me clean through the heart.

His lips twisted into a thin smile. "I know how to compromise."

I bit my tongue, holding back what was sure to be a smart ass retort, and nodded once. "Let's hit the road then. Daylight's a-wastin'."

He shook his head and turned, and I followed him outta Riley's apartment to his shiny new Ford F-150, crossing my fingers on the off chance I needed the extra luck to get through the day.

TRUE TO HIS WORD, Sheriff Treadwell stopped by Micky Dee's and bought us both some breakfast and hot, fresh brewed coffee.

I said not word one about it when he pulled out his wallet and handed the cashier at the window a crisp twenty-dollar bill. Some things was worth fussing over. This'un weren't.

Soon as we got our bag of food (piping hot country ham biscuits with sides of crunchy hash browns), the sheriff pointed his truck toward Helen. I didn't have to ask which way we was a-travelling. The fastest and best route from here to there was out Highway 76 West toward Hiawassee, then a sharp left onto GA-197 somewhat before we hit the Towns County line. The roads was curvy, but well-maintained to that point. Like as not, early morning traffic would be mostly folks headed to work or school.

The truck's cab was quiet 'cept for road noise and the music turned low on the radio. Classic Rock, same station I listened to out of Atlanta. Probably the only thing me and him had in common, save Riley and Ann, and I weren't right certain the good sheriff considered me a part of their lives.

Nobody'd mentioned it, but I reckoned he still held a grudge against Fame, and he didn't rightly seem like the sort to let go of bad blood.

When we got close, the sheriff parked at a gas station and pulled up the nature camp's address on Google Maps on his cellphone. "Damn thing takes you all over the goddamn countryside if you let it," he muttered under his breath.

I pressed my lips together real tight, hiding a smile. My phone weren't advanced enough for them apps or whatever they was, but I heard Riley fuss about this particular one ever time he had to use it. Me, I'da just used a paper map and been done with it.

Twenty minutes later, after the most haphazard route I seen in a while, we drove past a sign announcing that the Four Corners Nature Camp and Spiritual Retreat was the next right. Sheriff Treadwell slowed down and hit his turn signal, then eased the car onto an unlined paved road just wide enough for two cars.

The woods was thick here and full of young pine under a growing sun, but the longer we drove, the older the trees got and the fewer the new growth evergreens. The forest seemed to close in around us, edging toward the road like it was protecting the lane somehow, or maybe that was the voice inside me stirring uneasily.

After about a mile of seeing not a dadgum thing besides woods, the road curved around and over a small hill. There was the lodge sitting comfy and cozy behind a loop at the end of a roundabout, settled into a hollow that was narrow on this end and widened out the farther it stretched between the hills bracketing it.

The main lodge was bigger'n I remembered it being from the pictures I seen online, wider and taller both. Online, it'd looked like it was only about two stories high, but now I realized it was more like three, given the peaked Alpine looking roof at the front. Glass windows angled in along the front from the rock patio to the eaves up top around giant double doors made of solid wood. The lodge extended into a two-story wing on either side of the central structure, and beyond, marked pathways disappeared into the forest, occupied by small, scattered groups of people.

The sheriff followed the signs to visitor parking and backed his F-150 into a spot in the otherwise empty lot. I slid outta the cab trailing my jacket behind me and paused for a minute in the warm air. Why, it felt like it was already fifty degrees out, a sight warmer'n it was back home. We was still in the mountains, the foothills, really, but it sure didn't feel like it.

I shut the door and slipped my jacket on, and left it unzipped as I walked around the front of the truck and met the sheriff there.

His gaze was glued to the lodge and his skin was a little too pale under the determination carved into his face. "Let me do the talking."

I shrugged. Thing was, he could handle it however he wanted, but if I needed to talk, danged if I was gonna keep my mouth shut.

We walked side by side along the pavement edged by winter brown grass to the patio, skirted the bottom of a wooden ramp wedged against the lodge, and jogged up the shallow rock steps to the entrance. The sheriff pulled one of the doors open and waved me in, and I stepped into an open lobby extending some fifty feet back to a wall lined with more giant windows.

Two massive rock fireplaces bracketed the room to the left and right, just beyond hallways leading into the wings, each holding a brightly dancing fire. Brown leather sofas and chairs was placed in front of the fireplaces, with more furniture arranged in cozy groups in between and in front of the far windows. A few of the chairs held women of various ages and races with their noses buried in books. To the right, a group of three younger women sat in front of that fireplace, chatting quietly amongst themselves.

The ring warmed against my chest under the long-sleeved t-shirt I wore and a restless feeling stirred in my gut. I couldn't pinpoint the whys of it or the hows, so I tucked it away and tried to ignore it.

One of the women sitting in front of the fire looked up and noticed us, and her smile was so automatic and friendly, I couldn't help but smile back. She said something to her companions, then stood and walked toward us, her boot heels ringing on the dark-stained, hardwood floors. She was maybe my height and generously curved in the way some women was without carrying an ounce of unneeded fat. Voluptuous, I reckoned, like Missy, though this'un was blonde headed and looked for all the world like a college co-ed in her stylish cowl-necked sweater and jeans.

As she drawed nearer, though, I changed my mind about that. Her eyes was brown and deep and held the calm wisdom of a woman what'd been around long enough to see the world for what it was. Still, she held out her hands to us as she approached and her smile got brighter, if you can believe it.

"Welcome to our home in the woods," she said. Her voice was smooth and soothing, like water bubbling in a creek. Melodic, almost. "I'm Nora Vargas, Four Corners' manager. How can I help you?"

Sheriff Treadwell held out a hand and grasped hers like it was a rattlesnake trying to spit lightning at him. "Chip Treadwell. This is Sunshine Walkingstick. We have some questions about what you do here."

Nora shot a smile at me, then turned it on the sheriff. "I'm your gal, then. Why don't I give you a tour while you ask your questions?"

The sheriff nodded. "I could do with a walk."

I glanced at him outta the corners of my eyes. The drive down was long enough to need a good leg stretching, sure, but ten to one, that weren't why he agreed to Nora's tour. But hey, when an opening come along to poke around, why not take it, right?

"Great," Nora said, her voice so perky, she practically hummed with good will. "Just let me grab my jacket. It's a bit nippy outside today. Back in a jiff."

Ok, I admit it. I rolled my eyes just a little, couldn't help it. The last time I seen somebody so all fired happy, I was in high school watching Belinda Arrowood, then Heaton, and her ilk do their ra-ra-go-team at a football game. That hussy sorta put me off the whole fake cheerful crowd, though Nora seemed genuine enough.

Time'd tell.

Nora come hustling back into the main lobby two shakes after she stepped into her office, an unmarked door to my right. She slipped into one of them bubble jackets, a red one that perfectly offset her honey colored skin and rich blonde hair. All dolled up like that, she looked as svelte and pretty as one of them Victoria's Secrets models.

I tugged at the bottom of my own jacket, a denim number I'd had so long, I'd forgotten where I got it, and followed her and the sheriff back outside.

The morning air seemed to warm up on command the minute Nora entered it, like it was so happy to see her, it'd do anything for her.

Maybe that was my imagination, but there was something about her, something compelling. Then I noticed a soft warmth against my chest and remembered why we was there, and figured out it was a good bet pretty little Nora had some magic to her.

I shook my head and fell into step behind her and Sheriff Treadwell as she led us around the side of the lodge onto a series of mulch lined paths spreading out through the woods.

Her hand swept out to the left and her words seemed rote, like she'd done this song and dance a hundred times before. "The Nature Camp was founded in 1909 by a group of women from Atlanta who were looking for a retreat from the city's congestion."

"They ain't seen the half of it," I muttered.

Nora glanced over her shoulder at me, her mouth

curved into a smile I was beginning to think she was born with. "Nothing like today, of course, but we still come here for the same reason. To escape the pollution and crime and noise. To reconnect with Mother Earth and our inner spirits. For fellowship with like-minded companions."

"Sounds like poker night to me," Sheriff Treadwell said.

Nora laughed and faced forward. "Something like that. The original lodge was much smaller and constructed of timber logged from the surrounding forests. It burned in 1926, and for a decade the women chose to meet in a farmhouse located on the edge of the property."

I tuned the lecture out and focused on the surroundings instead, studying the lay of the land, the trees, and the odd person or two strolling along the paths. Most was women, sure, but a couple was men, and that took me aback somewhat. Wasn't witches of the female persuasion, or was that a stereotype at work in my noggin?

I made a mental note to check on that soon as we got back home.

One of them men passed us on the path, murmuring gruff niceties as he jogged by, and the ring's heat sharpened into a brief scorch. I tried to memorize his face, so's I could check him against that list of associates I dug up last night, but he was by me so fast, all I got was sharp features and bright green eyes and a dark scent so fleeting, I couldn't pinpoint its likeness.

Familiar, though. Whatever it was, I'd smelled it before, and recently, too.

Nora took us on a winding loop around the trails, her bright chatter punctuated by the sheriff's deeper drawl. I was so deep in my study of the property, I only caught the odd word or two, but one word jumped out at me and slung me right outta my communion.

Witch.

"Small town rumors," Sheriff Treadwell was saying, his voice deceptively mild.

Nora laughed and threaded her arm through his elbow, for all the world like they was the dearest of friends. "Pure rubbish. Of course, wiccans come here to practice the craft in peace or to cleanse their spirit, but dark magic?" She shook her pretty, blonde head. "An' it harm none. That's the primary vow of every practitioner."

"Sounds like personal experience," I said.

"It is," she said, just as easy. "I practice myself. There are no dabblers here, and no light-hearted followers. The Great Goddess smiles down upon us all."

We'd looped back around to the building by then without me realizing, though we was at the back entrance of one of the wings. Sheriff Treadwell stopped walking and faced Nora, his mouth open on what I was sure'd be a pointed question.

Just then, the back door opened and out stepped a tall, slender woman whose hair was bright as the noonday sun above a chunky, off-white sweater and jeans. A whiff of something tantalizingly familiar drifted to me and was gone as the ring flared to life against my skin and my head went dizzy with them dadgum symbols. The woman smiled a friendly enough smile, same as Nora, but there was something about her I couldn't quite put my finger on. Nothing bad, far as I could tell, just something different and old.

Nora dropped Sheriff Treadwell's arm and held out a hand to the new arrival. "Brenyn, you're just in time to meet our guests."

I suffered through introductions and the polite murmurs of the newcomer, but tucked my hands in the back pockets of my jeans, more outta instinct than my usual reluctance to touch strangers and kin alike.

"Chip and Sunshine were curious about our camp," Nora continued, once she'd called out ever body's name, her own smile firmly in place. "And as our historian, you're the perfect person to shed light on what I may have missed."

Brenyn clasped her narrow hands together in front of

her. "I'm certain you've missed nothing. Our Nora is quite thorough in her duties."

Her voice held the lilt of foreign origins, though danged if I could put my finger on that neither. That mysteriousness was beginning to bug the ever-loving daylights outta me. I shifted from foot to foot and glanced at the sheriff, and sharp man that he was, he took the hint and kept his questions short and to the point.

Not a word did he say about them missing young'uns. I reckoned that was all part of his plan.

Me, I woulda spilled the beans by now and maybe had somebody on the ground and a knife to their throat, but I weren't so subtle as him.

We left not long after, having learnt not a blessed thing, far as I could tell, except that some of them folks held a butt load of magic and some didn't.

Which left me wondering if they was all witches, or all wannabes, or somewhere in between.

The car ride home was silent and tense. When the sheriff dropped me off at Riley's around lunch, the only thing he said was thank you before he drove away, leaving me pretty dang clueless as to any conclusions he mighta drawed.

12

Soon as I got outta the sheriff's truck, I high stepped it into Riley's apartment and throwed my stuff together. On impulse, I grabbed that paper full of them symbols and shoved it into my overnight bag without looking on it too hard. It was past time me and Missy had a little come to Jesus talk about this whole witch business, and I didn't aim to let her slide by without getting me some answers this time.

I weren't in such a huge hurry I couldn't tidy up a bit as a thank you to Riley for letting me stay the night. It wouldn't take long nohow and I didn't want him to think I was an ungrateful git.

Besides. I liked doing for him. No sense hiding it anymore, was there?

I grinned to myself and hummed a tuneless song under my breath as I wiped down the kitchen counters, dusted the living room, and run a vacuum cleaner through both rooms and the bedroom. I was just winding the cord around the prongs on the back of the vacuum when the doorbell rung.

Now, who in tarnation was that?

I dropped the cord and jogged to the door, flung it open and grinned real big at the sleekly dressed woman standing there. "Howdy, Miz Treadwell."

Ann aimed a bare smile at me. "Hello, Sunshine. May I come in?"

"Well, it's your son's place. I don't hardly reckon you need an invite, do ye?" I stepped back anyhow and let her in, then shut the door behind her, closing out the winter wind whipping around the building. "I don't know what time Riley's getting off today. Ain't spoke to him since last night before bed."

"Oh, no, dear. I'm here for you. Do you mind if we sit?"

That puzzled me good, but I led her to the freshly straightened sofa and plopped down on one end. "You want something to drink or something?"

Ann sat gingerly on the edge of the sofa and perched her purse in her lap, holding it there with both hands. "I'm fine, Sunny, thank you."

I nodded and sat there for a minute, waiting for her to speak, studying her all the while. Ann Treadwell was a beautiful woman. Though she had to be over fifty, she didn't look a day past thirty-five, or wouldn't if her clothes wasn't so classy and fine. She was a polished diamond compared to her husband, though he weren't rough a'tall, just rugged. Still, I was thankful Riley took his looks and nature from her, and only his coloring and build from his daddy.

Just when I thought I was gonna have to ask, Ann cleared her throat and said, "Riley told me you and he had started having sex."

Heat flooded into my cheeks, and if I coulda slid under the couch, that's where mortification woulda sent me. But I was Fame Carson's niece, and by golly, weren't nothing gonna send me running if I could help it, so I looked her square in the face, red cheeks and all, and said, "Yes'm, that's true."

Ann's hands tightened on her purse. "Do you remember that day you saved him? All he talked about for days afterward was how this wild little girl snatched that snake out of the water and kept him from being bitten. He's adored you ever since."

The heat faded from my cheeks and I frowned at her. Sure, I remembered that day, though I for certain didn't know a thing about Riley adoring me. We was fast friends after then, sure. I reckoned that was natural, what with his mama nigh on adopting me from then on.

"Growing up," she continued, "I think he always believed the two of you would end up together, in spite of his father's views on your family."

I opened my mouth on a hot retort having to do with the sheriff, and Ann reached out and clasped her hand on mine, shutting off the venom rising up in me quicker'n spit.

"They're a wild bunch, Sunshine." Her voice was gentle and her eyes held what I coulda sworn was regret. "But I always knew you were different. I always thought you'd make him happy."

The first inkling of discomfort crept into me. "We was friends," I said, real careful.

"You were. For a while." Her hand slid off mine and returned to her white knuckled grip on her purse. Whatever her eyes'd held a minute before, it bled out and was replaced by the kinda cold I never seen in her before. "Then he found out you were pregnant with Henry. It was just a few weeks before his eighteenth birthday. His grades started dropping, he lost interest in sports. I caught him in Chip's liquor cabinet one day, but not before he'd gotten drunk as a skunk. The next day, after he'd sobered up, he talked me into giving him permission to enlist in the Army. I knew what had happened. I knew why he was upset, and I hoped his time away would help him get over you, but he never did."

My hands closed into fists in my lap against the sour-sick

feeling in my stomach. Riley'd never told me any of this, never even hinted at it, but I was beginning to see a pattern I didn't rightly like, and I weren't too sure I wanted to hear no more, neither. "Why're you telling me all this?"

"Because you need to know."

"I don't think Riley'd want you spilling his secrets like this."

Her lips tightened into a thin slash across her mouth, and for the first time in forever, she looked close to her age. "Too bad. He was in the hospital the day Henry went missing, you know. I volunteered at the school. Henry was a sweet boy, Sunshine. You did such a good job with him."

Politeness popped outta my mouth through habit more'n anything else, I was so stunned by what she was saying. "Thank you. I loved him dearly."

"I know you did, sweetheart. We all did. Such a precious soul." She sniffed once and blinked away tears, and her mouth relaxed into a bittersweet smile. "We heard the news about him going missing, then about his death, and you, well. You took care of that, didn't you, dear?"

Memory stirred like it always did, of finding Henry's blood on the trail between my trailer and Fame's, of the crazy mad what'd took hold of me that day, of taking my daddy's hunting knife and tracking the beast I thought'd got my boy and killing it dead with my bare hands.

Only, turns out it weren't that pooka what got my sweet, sweet baby. Was my own grandmama, out to keep her bloodline pure. Bitterness twisted inside me and I swallowed it down. I'd bear the scars she give me to the day I died, them on the outside where her claws raked my skin, and them on the inside from the life she took so needlessly.

I couldn't tell Ann that, though. Only a few people knowed what'd really gone on that day, and I didn't see no need to upset Riley's mama anymore'n I already had, so I looked her square in the face and said, real firm, "Yes'm, I sure did."

Ann nodded, like she'd knowed that all along. "As soon as I could get hold of Riley, I told him about our poor, dear Henry. He was getting ready to reenlist, but instead, he took a medical discharge, which he should've done anyway, if you ask me. He came home so he could be here if you needed him."

I shook my head slowly, and in the dull grief of remembering Henry and the fresh surprise of learning them things about the man I was dating, I fumbled across the divide stretching between me and Ann and clasped her hand in mine. "I didn't know."

Ann turned her hand over and gripped mine, palm to palm, and her other hand come over mine so she was holding me between her cupped hands. "He won't admit it, but he cares deeply for you, and you keep pushing him away and hurting him. He told me how you'd accused him of treating you like a whore, but I'm telling you, Sunshine, that's not the way he sees you at all."

I near about squirmed on the couch and that heat started rising in my cheeks again. Hadn't I already learnt that lesson well? Did I need it revisited to remind me of what a fool I been to doubt Riley in the first place?

"You cut him to the bone, honey, you really do, but now I'm asking you, one mother to another." Her hands tightened on mine and her eyes bore into me, cutting me as deep as she said I cut her son. "Please stop hurting him. It's so hard watching him chase after you only to come away with his heart bruised and broken. I just can't stand to watch it anymore."

"Miz Treadwell," I said, but she shook her head and closed her eyes, and danged if tears didn't roll down her powdered cheeks.

"I'm begging you, Sunshine. Either love him the way he deserves to be loved or let him go. Please."

I opened my mouth, hoping something appropriate would come outta my mouth, but the only thing I could do was croak out a soft, "I'm sorry."

"Seems to me you're apologizing to the wrong person." She let go of my hands and dug around in her purse, pulled out a sharply pressed hanky and dabbed it to her cheeks. When she looked at me again, her expression was as determined as her husband's was earlier in the day. "Now enough of that. I've said my piece and won't speak of it again. I expect you at family meals from now on, as long as you're seeing my son."

I knowed an order when I heard it and weren't too keen on feeling the raw side of her tongue again anytime soon. "Yes'm, I'll be there."

"That's my girl." She stood and looked down at me, her expression sweet and full of the love she'd give me since the day that snake come after Riley and I yanked it outta the water. "I know you're hard at work tracking down those missing children, so I won't keep you. Let me know if I can be of any help. That's such an awful shame. Those poor parents must be out of their minds with grief and worry."

She bent and bussed my cheek, engulfing me in the sweet flowers of her perfume, and let herself out while I sat on the couch feeling like I been run over by a Mack truck what'd come whistling by outta the blue.

I CALLED LIBBY and left a quick update on her answering machine, then dashed off an even quicker note to Riley and hightailed it back home. It weren't that I didn't wanna see him. Sure I did, and I coulda hung around 'til he got off work, maybe run up to Ingles and got some groceries and cooked for him or something.

But the plain truth that I'd had my fill of the Treadwell family for one day. All I really wanted to do was wallow in the peace and quiet of my own home for a bit.

Then there was that talk with Missy I was bound and determined me and her was gonna have.

So I snagged my overnight bag and hopped in the IROC

and away I went, shuttling through the winter day as quick as the law allowed.

Needn't've worried about Missy none, though, as she was walking down the trail betwixt my trailer and Fame's when I pulled into the parking area outside my roost. She had on sturdy hiking boots today to go with her jeans and Carhartt jacket, one of Fame's castoffs, I was sure, or maybe one of the boys. You could never tell with Missy. I knowed she had nice clothes and the money to buy more, but danged if she'd wear 'em around the house unless she had to.

I grabbed my bag off the front seat, slid outta the car, and waved real big at her as I slammed the door shut with my hind end.

Which reminded me. What with hanging out with Riley these past few months and eating regular like and all, my clothes was getting a mite too tight. Shoot, I was even getting some boobs to me, something I thought'd never happen. If I kept this gaining weight thing up, and Lord knowed I could stand another pound or two, I'd have to buy me a real bra and go up a size in my jeans. Not just yet, though. I reckoned a proper shopping trip could wait 'til BobbiJean and Jazz got back from their delayed honeymoon. Weren't nothing like hitting the mall to put my friend in a sparkling good mood. Maybe Missy'd tag along, too, so's I could just sit back and listen to 'em chatter instead of having to chatter away myself.

Missy glided right up to me and bussed my cheek real good, then she smoothed a bare hand over my messy ponytail, her violet eyes pinched with worry. "I heard you were out with Sheriff Treadwell today."

Small town gossip. Good Lord above, was there any escape from it?

I clutched her hand in mine and squeezed. "Come inside and I'll tell you all about it. Got some questions for you anyhow."

Missy's hand tightened on mine, stopping me before I could take a single step. "You found the coven, didn't you?"

"Coven?"

Her free hand fluttered in front of her. "The witches that kidnapped those poor missing children."

"Seeing as how you give the sheriff their address," I said, trying hard to keep my voice somewhere south of irritated, "I reckon you already got the answer to that question."

"Sunny, please. You don't know what you're dealing with."

"I'm getting a right good idea." My voice was a hair too tart, so I softened it and squeezed her hand again by way of an apology. "Come on in before you catch your death of cold."

We walked silently up the porch steps and into the trailer. Missy's feet stuck to the shag carpeting soon as she got inside. I left her there and dropped my overnight bag onto my bed, dug that paper out, being real careful to keep my eyes averted, and inched the heat up to a respectable temperature on my way back into the living room.

Missy was still standing there, looking lost as a lamb from its flock.

I stopped in the kitchen, put that paper facedown on the mosaic table where it could do no harm, and set about making coffee. "You ok, hon?"

She glanced up at me like a deer what'd jumped out into the road and was startled by the cars traveling the highway. "I'm fine. Here. Let me help."

She shed her jacket and hung it up, then joined me in the tiny kitchen area and hunted through the cabinets 'til she found Riley's stash of Oreos. She was reaching for a plate when my patience snapped.

"We can just eat 'em outta the bag like normal folk, Missy." I planted my butt against the counter and crossed my arms over my chest, eyeing her real good. "What's got into you anyhow? You're nervous as a honey-coated cat dancing across an ant mound."

Missy huffed out a tiny laugh and shut the cabinet door. "You have such a way with words, Sunshine."

"There's more where them come from. Since you're so fidgety, why don't you take a gander at that paper right there on the table."

The coffee starting bubbling right about then, so I turned to it and pulled out some clean mugs while Missy took the Oreos to the table and sat down. Paper rustled, then she hissed in a soft breath.

"Sunny, where did you find these?"

I shook my head. "Come to me while I was researching that address you give the sheriff."

"These are arcane. Ancient." Paper rattled again, the bag of Oreos by the sound of it. "Magic, even, some of them anyway. And they came to you while you were awake?"

"Wide eyed and bushy tailed." I paused the coffee maker and poured us two cups, then started it up again so it could finish brewing a full pot. I had a feeling I was gonna need it to get through the rest of the afternoon. "How come your ring don't get all hot and funny when you're around?"

She glanced up from the paper and paused with an Oreo halfway to her mouth. "What do you mean?"

"I mean, the only time it activates or whatever it does is when I'm around magic." I set a cup in front of her and sat down beside her, cupped the hot mug between my hands and stared her down. "It heated up plenty of times today, sometimes so hot, it nigh on scorched me."

She looked at the Oreo in her hand and sighed. "I do wish you'd let me put these out on plates."

"Stop stalling and spill the beans."

"Fine. It's a bit of a story, though."

I sat back in my chair, my gaze firm and even. "I got all day."

She placed the paper flat on the table and began turning the Oreo between the fingers of both hands. "Long ago, in the days when chivalry was young and new and the old kings ruled the lands, there lived a woman, an enchantress of great power. She was a companion to Merlin, a student of his really, and a healer of sorts, though she was learned in other magical arts."

"You talking about *the* Merlin? King Arthur and the knights of the round table and all that?"

Her eyes slid to mine. "Do you want to hear this story or not?"

I held my hands up and grinned. "Sorry."

"Hmph."

"Just one question, though."

She shook her head, sending the sable curls piled willy-nilly on top of her head bouncing. "Just one?"

"No, but just one for now. Is this enchantress you?"

The Oreo crumbled beneath her fingertips, but her gaze stayed steady on mine. "Yes."

That took me aback. I mean, I knowed something was going on with her. Nobody walked outta the woods looking like Missy did, back when she first come to us, but I always thought she was just an ordinary woman looking for an excuse to make a home, not some ancient witchy woman.

"I shoulda knowed," I murmured, then cringed. Them words weren't the ones I was meaning to say. I sucked in a deep breath and let it all out at once, then tried again. "On New Year's Eve when you banished Perchta. And before that, on the night the sheriff took Fame. Your hair, your eyes. They was plumb wild."

A small smile curved her pretty lips. "I was quite upset."

"I could tell." A tremor run through my own hands. I cupped 'em tighter around the mug and sipped at my coffee, aiming for a polite way to ask my next question. "How old are you?"

"I've forgotten," she said softly, then she brushed the cookie's crumbles into a pile and took up her own mug of coffee. "Centuries, maybe older. We didn't keep track of time back then the way humans do today. Seasons changed, kingdoms rose and fell."

"And you saw them all."

There was a note to my voice of awe and wonder, and

maybe more than my fair share of curiosity. That explained an awful lot, not just the way Missy acted, so calm and cool, but the scents I sniffed around her along and along, and sometimes the sounds, too. Fresh mowed grass. A musty tomb. The smell of blood on a sword and the clash and roar of a great battle.

I set all that aside and searched for a way to bring the story back around to where it needed to go. "King Arthur?"

"And Sir Gawain and..." She brought the mug to her lips, set it back down without drinking a lick from it. "That's how I came into possession of the ring, actually. It's a ring of legend, once possessed by Rogero, a nephew of Charles the Great. Tales have been told about it. You have one version on your shelves. I made sure of it."

Legends of Charlemagne, a Christmas gift one year not long after Henry died and it become clear to what was left of my family where my life was headed. I'd read it cover to cover more'n once. In that moment, sitting here with the woman what was as much a mother to me as the one what'd borned me, a particular tale popped into my head, of a ring what granted invisibility to the wearer and of a beautiful sorceress living in the time of Merlin.

"Melissa," I murmured, and now the awe was plain as day.

"Yes," she said, like she hadn't just admitted to knowing a wizard of so long ago, his name'd fallen into legend. "The ring came to me. It became my duty to protect it, and I have, but at a great price. As long as I carried the ring, I could never grow old, never die unless felled by a sword, never love."

One of her hands slipped under the table and pressed flat against her stomach, and my own blindness smacked me upside the head. "You're pregnant."

She nodded, and that hand clenched into a fist against her middle. "As long as I carried the ring, as long as I was its protector, I could never have a family of my own. Magic carries a heavy price, Sunshine, one I was willing to pay until the ring called me here to you and Fame."

I touched the ring, still tucked under my long-sleeved t-shirt. "You mean I can't get pregnant neither, long as I'm wearing it?"

"What price you pay for the magic is yours alone. No two bearers carry the same burden."

Questions buzzed around in my head, though I hadn't a clue how to name 'em, so I sipped my coffee and focused on the questions I come to the table with. "It tells me when somebody magic is around. Not you, but others. Libby sometimes and all of the painters, and ever once in a while other folk and monsters."

Missy leaned forward and speared me with a serious gaze. "When precisely?"

"In the woods with Spearfinger a little, but more when me and Libby was looking for them kids. We was on the trail and the ring..." My hands flapped in the air in front of me as my words trailed off. I couldn't explain what'd happened then, the twisting of magic upon magic, how the ring called to the beast I'd inherited from my daddy, that tiny part of him still buried deep in my soul. "Then today, it warmed around a couple of the people and got downright hot around some others."

"Who?" Her hands crept to mine and held me so tight, her fingernails dug into my skin. "Can you name any of them?"

"Nora Vargas," I said real slow, "and a man on the trail whose name I never caught, and another woman named Brenyn."

Missy paled and her hands went slack on mine. "Brenyn? Are you certain?"

"Yeah. Miss Nora introduced us, so I caught her name real good."

"No, it can't..." She hissed in a sharp breath, then slid off her chair and knelt beside me. "You must let this go, darling, let it go now and move on. There's nothing you can do for

116

those children."

I gawped at her like she'd slapped me with one of her narrow, elegant hands. "They's kids, Missy! You know how I feel about young'uns. I ain't leaving a single one in harm's way, if there's anything a'tall I can do to save 'em."

"There's nothing you can do. If Brenyn is involved…" Her face crumpled into worry and she buried it against my side. "She'll kill you, Sunshine, you and everyone you ever loved. Chances are good those children are already dead, too. Please don't sacrifice your life for those who can't be saved."

"But Missy," I said, then clamped my lips shut. Protesting weren't gonna do a cussed thing to change her mind, nor mine, neither one. But there was things I needed to know, things Missy could tell me, and I aimed to get as much outta her as I could. "This Brenyn. Is she a sorceress like you?"

"A black hearted witch," she said, her voice bitter cold. "Nothing like me."

"She's up to no good."

Missy let out a tired lap, then pushed away from me and stood. "Brenyn came out wrong, a consequence of the conditions surrounding her birth. There's nothing you can do to stop her, but be warned, darling. Where Brenyn goes, her brothers are sure to follow."

"Brothers?"

Missy shook her head and turned away from me, heading toward the door. "I need to start supper now. Fame and the boys have been out in the woods all day. They'll be cold and hungry when they come down the mountain."

I stood and stayed where I was, trembling like a leaf with the table my only support. "Missy, you know I can't let this go."

She paused with her back turned to me and one hand on the worn coat that had somehow become hers and hers alone. "I know, darling. Supper will be at six if you're hungry. Bring Riley. He's always welcome at my table."

"Missy," I said, though whether it was a plea or a question, I couldn't ken. She wrapped the coat around her shoulders and slipped out the door, so quiet, the only tale of her passing was the squeaking of hinges against the winter wind.

13

The rest of the day was about as restless as a day could get. After Missy left, I just couldn't stand them questions still buzzing around in my head, for all the world like buzzards what'd spotted fresh road kill, so I throwed my jacket on, scrounged for work gloves, and spent an hour and a half outside doing whatever chore come to mind. I picked up branches outta the yard and dumped 'em in a pile for Trey to help me burn, raked a good load of mulch out along the trail, and spread some more out at the little memorial garden me and Missy'd put together over the years along the site where I found Henry's blood.

And that's about when all the energy drained outta me in one fell swoop. I staggered over to the bench and flopped into it, pulled my gloves off and laid 'em on the bench, and sat there panting into the late afternoon air. The sun was a pale orange ball hovering just above the tree line, throwing shadows over me and the trail.

I shivered and tucked my hands between my arms and my sides and huddled there while my heart slowed down and I caught my breath.

A warm wind blowed around me, too warm for the time of year, rousing me from my frenzy induced stupor. *Mama*, it seemed to say, but it weren't Henry's voice reaching out to me. Leastwise, it weren't the voice I remembered him having, and of a sudden, Old Mother's words of a few months back come to me, how she shook and shimmied on my porch and her voice deepened into a demon's, and the warning she imparted to me about my boy.

Mama, the wind said again, and a chill snaked down my spine, raising goose bumps on my flesh. I looked into the wind and the woods, searching for my boy, or what was left of him.

"Henry," I said, though my voice wavered and wobbled.

"Mama," came the reply in my baby's sweet tones, then more plaintive like, "Mama."

I reached a hand out to the wind, holding it there while warmth surrounded me. "I'm here, baby."

Under my hand, the leaves stirred into a dervish, spinning 'round and 'round at my feet. Acorns tumbled along the mulch spread around the tiny angel marking the very spot where I found Henry's blood, then joined the leaves whirling 'round. I tried to draw my hand back, but something held me there, held me in place while nature's detritus spilled together in a giant jumble of browns and grays.

"Sunny!"

The voice jogged me out of whatever spell I was under. I jerked my arm back and glanced up at Trey running down the trail, his boots heavy on the dirt, a plastic bag held in one hand, a flashlight in t'other. Night had fallen while I was sitting there and the chill bit into me so hard, my knees clacked together as I shivered.

Trey slid to a stop beside me, dropped the bag on the

ground, and wrapped himself around me on the bench. "Good God, Sunny. What're you doing out here in the dark?"

I curled my fingers into his shirt and shook my head against his broad chest, so scared spitless, the words bottled themselves up in my throat.

"Sh," he murmured against my hair. "I got you now. Sh."

I didn't realize I was crying 'til I shifted against him and hit a wet spot in his shirt. I pulled back a mite and sniffed down the tears, rubbed my nearly numb hands down my jeans. "What're you running down the trail for?"

"You missed supper. Missy sent me down with a plate." He stooped and snagged the bag in his hands. The light from his flashlight slid along the ground, and he froze half bent over. "Good God. What is that?"

I glanced down and froze, just like him. On the ground where that dervish'd been was a mosaic of acorns and stones and God alone knowed what else, patterned to make a picture. It was a good likeness, for all that it was made of discarded parts, and it shot horror through me like that voice whispering to me shoulda done.

"Is that...a painter?" Trey said, his voice half an octave higher'n normal.

I pulled my cellphone outta my pocket. "Shine that light a little closer, wouldja?"

He obliged and I took a picture, but I didn't need it to remember what I seen. Henry, or whatever had spoken to me, had created the very likeness of a painter's face.

I didn't know what to make of that. Was he reminding me what really killed him? Or was he warning me of something yet to be?

Trey looped the bag's handles onto his fingers under the flashlight and wrapped an arm around my shoulders. "C'mon, sis. Let's get you warmed up and some hot vittles in you."

I let him tug me away without comment, knowing that to the day I died, I'd remember that acorn and stone mosaic without having to look on the picture I took even once.

TREY STAYED long enough to make sure I et, then he all but shoved me down the hallway toward the shower on his way out the door. Soon as I dried off and done my nightly ablutions, I pulled on one of Daddy's old t-shirts and climbed into bed. Sleep took me about the same time my head hit the pillow, and if dreams visited me, they was long gone when I woke up bright and early the next morning knowing exactly where the day would take me.

I jumped outta bed, did the necessaries, and rushed into the living room toward the lone bookcase where I kept research books. The tome I needed was on the top shelf, tucked between *Grimm's Fairy Tales* and a threadbare copy of *Le Morte d'Arthur*. *Legends of Charlemagne* by Thomas Bulfinch, the book Missy give me one Christmas past.

I scanned through 'til I found the tales concerning her and the ring, then I sat down at the kitchen table and read, focusing on how the ring was used. Some folks used it to sneak around unseen, but Melissa, the one in the story, kept saying it was some kinda talisman against enchantments.

I pulled the ring outta my shirt and fingered it, my mouth turned down in a frown. I couldn't say nothing about neither one of them things. I'd never put the ring on. Missy'd warned me about that right off, and maybe that's why, 'cause she didn't want me being invisible for some reason.

But if the ring had the power to overcome enchantments, like the tales said it did, then how come I kept being bedazzled by whatever was going on at Henry's little spot on the trail?

Once I was done reading, I closed the book, using my finger to mark the spot I'd left off, and stared into the distance, my eyes unfocused while I pondered the story. Missy was a witch. That's what I kept coming back to. It's not like I didn't understand why she hadn't told us. I mean, what woman in her right mind would admit to such, even in this day and age?

Which brung me right back to the folks me and the sheriff seen at that nature camp. They wasn't out in the open, exactly, but they wasn't exactly hiding their natures neither. Nora'd come right on out and said she was practicing the craft, though she swore up and down, seemed like to me, that she weren't hurting a soul.

Yet Missy'd said that Brenyn was old and...how'd she put it exactly? I thunk back and finally landed on the exact words. A black-hearted witch.

So if Miz Nora was such a goody two shoes, what was she doing consorting with the likes of Brenyn?

I didn't know, but I aimed to find out.

My stomach growled a protest right about then, so I marked my place in *Legends of Charlemagne* with a scrap piece of paper, re-shelved it, and set about making a scramble outta some frozen, cooked sausage and some fresh eggs. Half an hour later, I'd eaten and cleaned up, stuffed my notes on the abductions into a backpack, and was on my way down the road toward the White County Public Library in Cleveland, not too far from Helen and the nature camp. I wanted to know exactly what I was up against before I visited again and the only places I knowed where to look was in a book or on the internet.

Sadly, the library's only book on witchcraft was thirty years old and seemed to be based more on rumor and superstition than fact. I borrowed a computer instead, using my PINES library card, same one I showed at my home library, and hunkered down for a good looksee.

Half an hour later, I was just as confused as ever. For one, I couldn't find hide nor hair of no historic witch named Brenyn. Maybe she changed her name, or maybe she was just careful to keep herself hid, the way witches of old used to do to keep from being burned or hung or whatever other tortures people cooked up back in the day.

Modern witches wasn't devil worshippers, though. That much I found out, which begged the question as to what other kind of dark magic required the sacrifice of a child's life.

Or, in this case, multiple children.

I sat back in my chair and tapped a finger against the desk holding the computer. Maybe I had it all wrong, though. Maybe whoever'd kidnapped them kids was using 'em for some other purpose. Lots of folks was desperate for children they couldn't have on their own, not to mention them what got their jollies from having sex with young'uns. So many reasons why them kids mighta been kidnapped popped into my head, I finally signed off the computer and left the library.

It weren't quite lunchtime by then, so I hopped in the IROC and pointed it toward the nature camp. If I hurried, I could catch Nora just before she took her own meal break, when her belly was empty and her guard was down. Maybe I could rattle her enough to get her talking on what them witches was really up to down Helen way.

NORA WAS right where we found her yesterday, sitting on a couch in front of a flickering fire, only this time she was alone, though her outfit hadn't changed much. Today's sweater was a rich purple against her jeans. Her legs was curled up under her and her head was bent toward a thick stack of papers resting in her lap.

I marched right across the lobby, not even trying to hide the clack of my boots on the hardwood floor, and plopped myself onto the sofa just opposite her.

She glanced up, smiling automatic like, then her smile softened into recognition. "Hello, Sunshine. To what do we owe the pleasure of your visit?"

I liked a woman what got right to the point, so much so that I reached into my backpack and pulled out my own stack of papers, the folder of them missing kids. "I got some questions."

"I thought you and Sheriff Treadwell covered everything yesterday."

That took me aback. We hadn't told her who we was. I didn't bother to ask how she knowed, though. If I was in her position and two strangers come sniffing around my place of business, I'da looked into 'em, too.

"I always got more questions," I said instead and pulled out one of the reports, this'un for Sophie Whitehead. I hadn't meant to pull out Henry's sister, but if that was the way fate wanted to play it, I was just fine discussing her. "We got some kids gone missing in this area. Some of the parents hired me to track 'em down when the police give up looking for 'em."

Sympathy flickered over Nora's expression, and I coulda swore it was genuine. "I'm sorry to hear that. How can we help?"

"You can tell me which one of you took 'em, that's what."

She blinked at me, just once, then her expression turned to granite. "I told you yesterday. We're peaceful people, intent on harming no one. It's one of our basic tenets."

"Maybe yourn," I retorted, "but not ever body. I smelled the red magic around where them kids disappeared, and unless I'm mistaken, I smelled it again yesterday on some of your people."

That was a bit of a stretch, but what the hey. What I'd got from that man on the trail and from Brenyn coulda just as easy been dark magic and my sniffer weren't good enough to tell the difference. Which is what I got for not bringing Libby's sharp nose along.

"Red magic..." Nora said, then her eyes widened and her skin paled a shade under her natural tan. "You're talking about blood magic. We don't do that here. No one would. To use blood magic would be..."

"A sin?" I said into the gap she left. "You sure nobody here'd do that?"

"Of course not. Why would we? The only reason

someone would have to use blood magic would be..." Her voice trailed off again and she shook her head. "Nothing good. I can't imagine anyone who'd—"

"Anyone who'd what?" I prompted.

She shook her head again, sending her honey blonde hair sliding around her shoulders. "Nothing. No one."

"No, don't stop now. What was you a-thinking?"

"I wasn't thinking anything." She gathered her papers together and stood. "Now, if you'll excuse me, I have work to do."

I stood right along with her. "Oh no, you don't, missy. You know somebody's up to no good or you wouldn'ta hesitated."

She huffed out a small breath. "I have no idea—"

"Don't feed me no line of bull," I said, suddenly so fed up, I coulda spit. The ring flared to life then, feeding off my mad maybe, but whatever it was, a surge of something electric flowed through my veins, lighting me up inside and out. "You tell me what you know about them missing kids."

My voice come out all growly, like the painter had ahold of me, what little was in me. Nora's hands tightened on her sheaf of papers, but to her credit, she stood her ground, facing me down like she seen worse'n me on her best day and weren't afraid to see it again.

"What are you?" she said.

"Determined." I cleared my throat, shook my head, and just like that, the painter let me go and I was plain ol' Sunshine again. "You gonna help me out or not?"

Her expression melted from wary curiosity into regret. "If I could help you, I would."

"You can help." I yanked up Sophie's report and held it up where Nora'd get an eyeful. "She ain't but six years old. You want her blood on your hands?"

A clatter of footsteps tumbled into the building right then, ringing across the lobby like it was a herd of elephants rather than the few people I could feel at my back. Witches ever one, by the buzzing glow of the ring against my skin.

"We felt magic," a familiar voice said.

Nora's bourbon colored eyes slid from me to the newcomers and she held up a hand. "Everything's fine. Just a little misunderstanding."

"Ain't no misunderstanding." I turned and held up Sophie's report where the four women what'd entered could see, Brenyn being one. "I got me a slew of missing young'uns. Any of you know anything about that?"

Brenyn stepped forward, her expression stone cold. "You have no right to come here and make accusations like that."

"I ain't accusing nobody of nothing," I retorted. "But if I was gonna accuse, I'd start with you. Ten to one, you ain't told this bunch half the truth of what you are."

Nora's hand wrapped around my arm and she murmured, "Don't, Sunshine. This isn't the time or the place."

Her words sparked instinct. *Danger*, it whispered, and I finally realized exactly what kind of knothole I'd forced myself into. Now, I weren't no coward. Nobody could accuse me of such. But I knowed when I was outnumbered and outgunned, and this was one of them times.

I shrugged Nora's grip off, though she meant it kindly, and stuffed Sophie's report into my folder. "Another kid goes missing and I'll be back here knocking in some teeth, you hear me?"

The women standing behind Brenyn started murmuring to themselves. Even where I stood, across the great expanse of the lobby, I could make out their words, things like "Just because we're witches" and "She's got a lot of nerve" and "Another witch hunt."

I weren't on no witch hunt, though. I just wanted to know where my boy's baby sister'd got off to. The answer was here. I could just about taste it in my mouth, mingling with the bite of something I couldn't quite place.

I strode out just like I always done, head held high, boots firm on the floor. When I walked past Brenyn, I paused and looked her straight in the eye. She looked back, too, and from what I seen, she knowed exactly what I was.

While we was standing there measuring each other, I took a good sniff, searching for that red magic or something of its kin, but whatever scent she held, my nose couldn't sort it from the other women's perfumes.

Dang my hide for not bringing Libby along.

Brenyn arched her eyebrows and stared down her nose at me as the other women spread out around us, their gazes an odd mix of hostile and curious. I looked at each one in turn, taking my feel of 'em so's I could describe 'em to Missy later, then nodded and moved on. I'd done what I come here to do and that was all what could be done, 'til I had something better to go on besides hunches and magic scents and the word of a centuries old witch.

I slapped one of the double doors open and walked to my car without looking back, but the sting of eyes boring into my back followed me across the parking lot and lingered all the way down the long drive toward civilization.

14

My mad lasted about ten minutes, maybe less. Before I even got back to the main drag, I started shaking like a leaf in a hurricane. Stupid, is what it was, walking in on nearly half a dozen witches like that with nobody at my back. Then goading 'em 'cause I was apparently too strung out on painter to keep my mouth shut.

Hellfire, I was a pure plumb fool.

I pulled over at the first fast food restaurant I seen and sat in the parking lot with my forehead touching the steering wheel between my hands, waiting for the shakes to leave me and my heart to calm down. Acid roiled around in my gut, threatening to shoot up my throat into my mouth, and clammy sweat broke out along my skin.

God a'mighty, what was wrong with me?

After my boy died, I spent years charging head first into danger without thinking twice on it. Weren't nothing different now. I was still the same stubborn mule. I still had a righteous need to avenge the weak and do right by them what done right by me. So why did confronting a handful of witches, however good or bad they was, have me sitting in a parking lot trying not to puke my guts out?

My phone beeped once, twice. I inhaled real deep, let it out slow, and fumbled my phone outta the seat beside me. Riley'd texted me. I knowed soon as my hand hit the phone who it was, and knowed too what was different now.

I had somebody to live for.

Danged if tears didn't well up in my eyes right along with the relief and happy and fondness welling up in my gut. When Henry died, I was so alone. Ever body else'd had somebody but me. Henry'd been my touchstone, the love what kept me sane, and when I lost him, maybe I lost that sense of connection with the rest of the people what loved me. Even Fame and Missy and the boys hadn't been enough to ground me, and Mama being in prison didn't help none neither.

But now I had Riley and I weren't so alone no more. I had somebody to care for me, somebody what fussed when I come back from a hunt all battered and bruised, somebody to fuss over in kind. It weren't just me I was risking when I dived into a bad situation. It was him, too.

His mama's words come back to me then, clear as a bell. *You cut him to the bone, honey, you really do.* Sitting there in the car with my phone cradled between my shaky hands, I realized that ever cut I took, ever fist, ever blow, Riley took, too, and when he took 'em, it hurt him same as it hurt me.

I didn't wanna hurt him no more.

A laugh trembled outta me, thin and weak and ragged, and I let them tears flow as long as they needed to. Let the people walking by wonder what'd got into that crazy woman sitting in her daddy's IROC. Weren't no never mind to me, not now and not ever again.

SOON AS I pulled myself together, I checked Riley's texts. The first was asking me to meet him for lunch and the second was some lovey dovey. I texted him back right away and let him know where I was and how long it'd take me to get home.

Almost immediately, he texted back. *Got off early today. Meet me at my place. Muah, you hot ball of loving.*

I grinned down at my phone. Two guesses what he wanted to do on his afternoon off.

This gal needed some fuel if she was gonna have an afternoon siesta with her number one feller. I hopped outta the car and about glided into the restaurant, used the necessary quick as I could, then ordered me a number seven from the counter.

To go, seeing as how I had somewhere else to be.

That said, I decided to take the long way home, from Helen to Clarkesville, then up Highway 441 to Clayton. It weren't really that much longer than t'other way, but I needed to clear my head and batten down the hatches before I seen Riley.

Well more'n an hour later, I pulled into the parking lot at his apartment building, and you know the first thing I seen? Belinda Arrowood's Lexus parked right beside Riley's Range Rover.

The breath hissed outta me like I been sucker punched.

I parked on t'other side of the lot in somebody else's spot and, for the second time that day, rested my forehead on the steering wheel. Just when I was getting used to him, Riley had to go and tomcat around on me.

That no good son of a cock sucking goat.

Darkness twisted up in me and my vision dimmed, and that instinct, the one what'd been hounding me here of late, nigh on yelled at me inside my own dadgum head.

Stop.

It took me a minute to figure out what it meant, but when I did, I was ashamed of my kneejerk reaction. Riley cared for me too much to cheat on me. We was friends, at least, and like his mama said, he'd been a good friend as long as I knowed him. And we was lovers, too, something Riley didn't take lightly. He weren't fooling around on me, no sirree, but that didn't mean I could trust that hussy not to try to drive a wedge between us.

It wouldn't be the first time she done it, that's for sure.

This time was the final straw, though. This time, Riley was mine and I weren't aiming to let him go no time soon. That hussy'd been coming between me and Riley for so long, I done lost count. I was sick of it, too, so sick my first instinct was to hold her down and squeeze the ever-loving life outta her.

I woulda done it, too, if I hadn't knowed exactly what'd happen to me for murdering somebody, however much it needed doing. Weren't my own mama in jail for the same sin?

I let go of the steering wheel and sat up, and if fire coulda shot from my eyes, it woulda. Little miss Belinda needed a lesson in manners where another woman's man was concerned. I sure didn't mind giving it to her neither.

Outta the car I went, like a shot, and up the stairs to Riley's apartment. I didn't bother banging on the door, just tried the doorknob, which turned out to be unlocked, and walked right on in like I owned the place.

Riley was leaning a hip against the couch, his arms crossed over his chest, smiling a half smile down at Belinda. She had her platinum blonde head tilted to the side and one hand resting on his forearms.

I slammed the door behind me loud enough to wake the dead and pasted a mile wide smile on my own mug. "Howdy, there. Didn't realize you had company."

Which was about the biggest whopper I told that week, but so what? I already owed my cussing jar for my meltdown earlier. What was one more quarter in the pot?

Belinda jerked around like a snake'd bit her and her baby doll mouth formed a perfect oh.

Riley glanced up and his smile turned into a grin. "Hey, baby. How was the drive?"

"Mighty fine, darling. I gotta wonder, though, why you're letting another woman put her hands on you when me and you had a play date scheduled for right about now."

Belinda sulled up and her mouth pinched into a disapproving moue. "Well, I never."

"And you never will, you sour-mouthed hussy," I said, sweet as sugar. "That's my feller there and I don't take kindly to poachers."

Riley had a hand over his mouth, and if I didn't know better, I woulda sworn he was trying not to laugh. "I love it when you get possessive."

I shot him a withering glare and opened my mouth to blister his hide good.

Fortunately for him, Belinda interrupted. "Riley told me he was looking for some property. I was just dropping off some brochures for him."

"Well, now that you have, here's the door." I half turned and put my hand on the doorknob. "I'll make sure it don't hit you on the way out, but only 'cause Riley don't like scenes."

Riley let out a guffaw and about doubled over with laughter. Belinda sniffed her nose and tottered toward me on four-inch heels, her steps short and minced thanks to the tight cut of her baby blue suit. She paused beside me and sniffed again, but I already had the door open, leaving her nothing to do but walk through it.

Good riddance, says I.

I shut the door and locked it, then turned some of my mad on Riley. "Don't you ever let that viper in here again."

"C'mon, Sunny," he said, all his laughter gone, but I held up a hand, stopping him short.

"Is you my feller or ain't ye?"

His expression softened. "I am, baby. You know that."

"Yes, I do," I said, surprised by the firmness of my conviction. I knowed he was mine, knowed it from one limb to t'other and ever where in between. That didn't mean I was gonna let him off the hook where Miss Snotty was concerned. "I mean it, Riley. You stay away from her. She's caused enough trouble between us."

"Sunny." My name was a long sigh on his lips. "What am I gonna do with you?"

"Love me."

The words sprung outta my own mouth unbidden, but once they was out, I couldn't take 'em back. More, I didn't wanna take 'em back. He opened his arms to me, and I ran right into 'em, jumping up so he caught me to his chest and buried his face in my throat.

"I do, baby," he murmured, then he kissed me soundly and I forgot all about the mad what'd drove me into his apartment in the first place.

15

I spent the next coupla days covering old ground and new. Me and Libby visited a few more of the places where kids disappeared, mixed in with ones we done seen, and come up with not much more'n what we already knowed. The trails stopped cold each and ever time. That red magic smell lingered along and along. And Missy's ring flared hot against my chest when it did.

I tried not to worry over much about the coupla hours of lost time spent at Henry's memorial spot, tried harder not to worry on Missy being a witch.

The things you learned about a body, just when you thought you knowed 'em inside and out.

Them symbols haunted me a bit, though, and weren't nothing I could do about it. I tucked the paper away amidst all my research on witches, a growing pile of notes and references sorted into files the best I knowed how. Still dreamed about 'em though, or rather, they popped up in my dreams and I remembered 'em the next morning.

Didn't know what they meant, couldn't find 'em on the internet, and Missy weren't talking.

Nobody was talking, as a matter of fact, not her, not the sheriff, not nobody. I'd hit a wall good. Truth be told, the whole affair rested heavy in my gut, gnawing away at me to *hurry, Sunny, hurry.* Time was running out. I could feel it in my bones. If them kids wasn't dead already, they was gonna be soon and weren't nobody looking for 'em no more but me and mine.

That Friday, Riley drug me outta the trailer and into town for a night out. "Whether you want to take one or not," he said, and much as I hated to admit it, the break'd do me good.

We washed up at his apartment, then hit the road searching for a restaurant we hadn't visited three times over since Thanksgiving, and landed at Ishy's, my favorite Mexican restaurant in Clayton.

No offense to t'other Mexican restaurants. I just liked the loaded potato soup, and sometimes they'd make up a fresh batch of peanut butter ice cream or a rich chocolate cake for dessert. I liked ending my meal on a high note.

After, we hightailed it to Franklin and the movies. Riley was a big movie goer and, like when a football game was on, I didn't mind tagging along with him. You just can't beat snuggling up to your feller in front of the big screen with a tub of popcorn shared between you.

I was doing ok letting the movie wash away my worries over them young'uns, Sophie in particular, 'til about halfway through the movie when a little niggling worm started working its way through my brain, disrupting my focus, and an ache set up residence in my tummy. Not a tummy ache like I ate something bad, but an ache like something bad was about to happen. I tuned out the action sprawling across the screen and the crunch of popcorn and Riley's arm around me, listening close to that inner voice what'd been growing so strong of late.

Nothing.

But the ache stayed in my gut, growing worse and worse, 'til by the time we got home around midnight, my nerves was strung so tight I thought they was gonna snap.

Me and Riley took turns in his bathroom, then cut the lights off and climbed into bed together. He curled himself around me and buried his face in the nape of my neck and said, "Night, baby," real soft. Two minutes later, he was a heavy, sleeping lump behind me and I was stuck staring into the darkened room, waiting for something to happen.

That lasted about five minutes before I had enough. For crying out loud! I had to get up early the next morning and do something about finding them kids. Didn't matter that I didn't know what to do except maybe round up the sheriff and Libby and go back down to the nature camp. I was gonna do something and that's all there was to it.

With that settled, I snuggled back into Riley and closed my eyes, ignoring that funny ache in my gut. I was a grown woman. I had responsibilities and duties and stuff, and weren't no bad feeling gonna stop me from—

Symbols danced in front of my eyes, superimposed against a moon dark forest, like when Neo was tapped into the matrix and watching it scrawl out across his mind. Some of the symbols was red, others was blue. They was lots of colors, as a matter of fact, and I wanted to touch 'em, taste 'em, bring 'em into me.

The forest behind 'em beckoned, though, so I pushed through the symbols like they was a curtain of strung beads and stepped barefoot onto the forest floor. The ground was cold beneath my feet and pine needles jabbed gently into my soles. Fog swirled around me, climbing up my legs, and in the distance, a painter screamed sharp and fierce.

Shadows moved through the winter bare trees, ghostly hands slid around rough bark, and a face flickered into view to my left. A little boy, stout and strong, with ears so big, he coulda flown.

Henry.

I stretched out a hand, but he laughed and skittered away, running ahead of me through the forest.

Catch me, Mama.

Some of the tension bled from me and I smiled. Why, it'd been a 'coon's age since me and my boy played hide and go seek, and why was that? We loved playing games together, Yahtzee and Go Fish and such, and we loved hiking through the woods around the trailer.

We should get back to doing them things again, shouldn't we?

The idea seemed right, but also wrong, and I couldn't place my finger on the whys.

No matter. That was my boy and I loved him deeper'n the deepest ocean. It was gonna be me and him forever, mark my words, just me and my boy and—

A painter strolled onto the trail in front of me and set itself between me and Henry. Its eyes was bright green, unnatural. It lowered its head as it stared at me, issuing a challenge, and I leaned down real slow and felt my ankle, searching for Daddy's knife.

Another scream pierced the night, close by, and my heart leapt into my throat. The painter twisted around on the trail and broke into a run, headed straight for Henry. Panicked now, I scrambled to follow, my feet pounding on the ground in time with the rapid thump of my heartbeat.

Henry, I screamed. *Watch out!*

He turned around and looked at me, his big brown eyes solemn, only it weren't Henry no more. It was Wyatt, Libby's middle boy.

Them symbols burst to life around him, glowing hot red and orange, licking at his skin like flames on firewood, consuming him bit by bit 'til only his eyes was left. Painter's eyes, green and unnatural, and familiar, oh, so familiar.

A woman laughed, triumphant, and the fire that was Wyatt separated into thirteen pieces, each a tiny, glowing flame shaped like a heart. The scent of cloves and graveyard dirt and death rose up around me, filling my mouth with every breath, and I choked and coughed as I held my hands out to the burning hearts, trying so hard to save 'em, trying so hard as the red magic filled my lungs and the flames touched my skin and burned through nerves and muscle and bone—

I screamed and sat straight up in bed, the covers held to my breasts. My skin prickled where the dream flames had burned me and tears streamed down my face, even as the dread what'd consumed me all night long finally come to a head.

Riley sat up beside me and yanked me straight into his lap against his chest. "What's wrong, baby? What happened?"

"Wyatt," I gasped out. "They got him."

"What?"

"The witches, Riley. They got Libby's boy."

My phone rang then, startling us both, and I scrambled off Riley's lap and grabbed it, fumbling the call open with shaky hands. "Libby?"

"It's Johnny," my granddaddy said. "You know."

I swallowed hard and closed my eyes as Riley slid off the bed and cut the bedside light on. "Yeah, I know. I'll be there soon as I can."

"Hurry, Sunny. We need you."

I ended the call and dropped the phone, trembling so hard, my teeth chattered. It was real, what'd happened in my dream. Not all of it, no, but the core of it, the essence. Why hadn't I put it together before, when my gut first started telling me something was wrong? Why hadn't I done something earlier before my little cousin was took from his own home?

Better, why'd I gone and poked a hornet's nest and put my whole family at risk? Missy'd warned me to leave well enough alone. She told me Brenyn was dangerous, but had I listened? No, I had not, and now look what'd happened.

Riley knelt in front of me, his body bare except for his boxer briefs. "Do you want me to call Dad?"

I looked at him for a minute, just sat there and stared, and finally shook my head. "No. I need to get there, though."

"I'll drive."

I sniffed once, twice, then a sob burst outta me and I flung myself at him. "This is all my fault, Riley, ever bit of it."

He shushed me and murmured soft words denying it, but no matter what he said, the truth clung to me in a thick fog of regret and fear.

RILEY DROVE as fast as the night'd allow him, one hand on the steering wheel, t'other on my thigh. I huddled in the seat, curled up facing him, cursing my stubborn hide for ever mistake I made over the past coupla weeks.

The Panther Clan was targeted because of me. Brenyn knowed what I was. Shoot, ever body down in that nature camp likely did after the stunt I pulled.

What was wrong with me? Why'd I keep going off half-cocked all the damn time?

Cars was parked up and down both sides of the street near Libby's house and the lights was on in half the neighborhood. Soon as Riley wedged the Range Rover between an aging pickup and a shiny new Lexus sedan and shut off the engine, I jumped out and half run, half skated across the frost slick grass.

Johnny opened the door before I could even knock and stepped back, silently inviting us in. A dozen or so people was crammed into the room, sitting in chairs where space allowed, all facing Libby and her husband on the couch, all elders in the Panther Clan. I knowed most of 'em now and could place names to faces and even kin to kin, including how they was related to me. These was my people, the half lost when Daddy married Mama against his mama's wishes. I weren't close with 'em yet, but Lord how I wanted to be.

That yearning could wait for another time. I studied Libby as Johnny cupped a hand on my shoulder, comforting me in his own way. My cousin's face was ashen and wet with tears and her eyes was dull, full of pain and sorrow and the kind of heart break I learnt only too well when my Henry was took from me so long ago.

My heart wrenched inside my chest. If Riley hadn't come up behind me then and blocked my way, I woulda stepped right back outside again.

This was all my fault.

Johnny shut the door behind us, and Libby looked up right then. Her face crumpled and she held out a hand to me, and next thing I knowed, I was sitting beside her, holding her while she cried into my shoulder.

"They took my baby, Sunny," she said, her voice broken by sniffles and sobs. "I don't know how, but they took him."

I glanced up at Elijah's solemn face. "What happened?"

He shrugged as he rubbed a beefy palm across his wife's back. "Libby woke up in the middle of the night. Had a funny feeling, she said, and asked me to make sure the house was locked up while she checked on the boys. We've been careful since the kids...well, you know."

Oh, I knowed all right. It'd been me, I wouldn'ta let my kids go to school, let alone play in the back yard unsupervised, what with all them kids going missing. One by one, they was took, a young'un here, another there, and nobody'd found the pattern 'til Terry Whitehead showed up on my porch and asked me to look for little Sophie.

And I'd asked Libby to help, putting her kids in danger, though I never meant to.

My eyes slid shut and I turned my cheek into Libby's head. "The boys weren't in bed."

"Jacob and Charlie were," Elijah said. "But not Wyatt. Libby came back out and told me his bed was empty, the pillow was still warm. And I already knew the back door was unlocked, though my hand to God, I locked it myself right after supper and checked again at bedtime."

Libby sniffed a final time and straightened away from me amidst the soft murmurs of kinfolk. "I checked it, too. Not because I don't trust Elijah. I just had this feeling. I needed to make sure."

I nodded. Yeah, that's something I understood all too well, fat lotta good it done me. "Nobody woulda come in the house without you knowing."

Elijah shook his head. "No way. We would've heard."

"I think he left on his own," Libby said. "Wyatt. I don't know why, but I think he walked out the door and met somebody."

I glanced around to my granddaddy. "You searched for him?"

"Trail went cold." Johnny raised an arthritic hand, pointing at the wall behind the couch where me and Libby and Elijah sat. "Not twenty feet back. Just disappeared. We've got people out searching, but they ain't finding nothing."

By people, I reckoned he meant them of the Panther Clan, and by that, I reckoned he meant that whoever was out there walked on four legs instead of two. Sharper noses, better hearing, better protection against the frigid night. Humans got the raw end of the evolution stick, you ask me. I'd give just about anything to be able to use my senses the way my painter kin did.

We was all quiet for a while. The thermostat clicked in the hallway and the furnace cut on. Hot air rushed through the floor vents, warming the air, and somewhere, a clock chimed four times.

The silence rubbed me raw, coupled as it was with the guilt resting heavy in my heart. I took Libby's cold, cold hands in mine and said, "What can I do?"

She looked at me for a minute, and gradually, her shoulders straightened and the pain in her eyes turned into hard determination. "We know who took him. We have a good idea where he's being held. I say we stand and fight."

Agreements run around the room. I looked at Riley where he stood beside the door, his feet spread wide, his arms crossed over his chest. My oak tree of a man. Dark circles rested under his eyes, but danged if his expression didn't mirror ever body else's.

Right then, I remembered the danger he was in and I shot straight to my feet. In my rush to get down here, I forgot all about humans taking on the nature of the painter, if they was around the two-natured for too long. It was one thing for Riley to spend the evening taking supper with Libby and her family, but to be here among a passel of my kinfolk, and no telling how long we'd be here? Damn it all to hell and back. Where was my head?

He musta recognized the look on my own mug, 'cause as soon as I stood, he held out a hand. "I'm not going anywhere."

"But what if—"

"Forget it, sweetheart. I'm staying."

Johnny's mouth quivered into a half smile among the wrinkles. "He knows the risk, same as you."

I harrumphed and glared at the both of 'em. Maybe I woulda said something pointed if Libby hadn't grabbed my hand and tugged me back down.

"He'll be fine, Sunny," she said, real soft. "Besides, we need him."

"Well, so do I," I retorted, somewhat sharper'n I meant to. "And just so you know, getting Wyatt back ain't gonna be a walk in the park. For one, they're gonna know we're coming. That one woman, Brenyn. She can smell magic a mile away. I reckon a lot of 'em can, the ones with deep magic in 'em."

"So they're all witches," cousin Noel said. He was about the same age my daddy woulda been if Mama hadn't killed him, and darker skinned, like he worked in the sun all day. His hair was still black as night, though, and tied back into a long braid tossed over the collar of a thick plaid shirt. "I thought all the witches died out centuries ago."

143

"Burned out," somebody said, and a coupla folks nodded.

Missy hadn't been. Neither had Brenyn. Maybe it was like ever thing else. The instinct for survival was so strong, a body'd do anything to outwit death.

Like sacrifice a bunch of children in a dark ritual under the light of the moon.

I frowned as something niggled in the back of my mind. No, not the light of the moon. The full moon done passed us by. We was under a waning moon now, not far from the new moon, as a matter of fact.

And Brenyn was still gathering children.

"We don't got much time," I said, each word slow and precise as I dug out my cellphone. A few clicks later, I had the answer I was looking for, and it weren't a good'un a'tall. "Three days. That's the peak of the new moon. That's when the witches is gonna do it."

Libby's nails bit into my hand, digging out half moons in my skin. "We need to get him now, before they kill him."

I thought about them flames dancing in my mind, thirteen souls waiting for us to save 'em, and I shook my head. "No, they're gonna expect us to attack right away. We need to make a plan, gather our strength, and the night before the moon's light disappears from the sky, we do it, when they think they've gotten away with it. Two nights from tonight."

Ever body looked at me, and for a minute, I thought they was gonna string me up. Then Johnny nodded his silver head, and Noel, and one by one, all the other folks gathered there did, too.

Finally, Libby relaxed her grip on my hand. "It's settled. We live together, we die together. We stand as one, but we're going to get my son back."

I locked eyes with Riley as the words echoed in my heart, and in his hazel gaze, I saw something I never seen before. He'd took Libby's words to heart, same as me, and this time, he was standing beside me when I faced the monsters fate seen fit to throw at me.

I closed my eyes again, shutting out the heartache already rising in me. It was one too many things for me to think on right then, but if I could find a way, weren't nothing I wouldn't do to keep my Riley safe from the fight what lay ahead of me.

16

I couldn't stand to just sit and do nothing, so soon as I got the opportunity, I excused myself from the living room and slipped into the kitchen. Them painters what was out still searching for Wyatt would need something hot in their bellies when they come in from the cold. Sure, they was a-walking on four legs right now and protected somewhat by fur, but that didn't mean they couldn't feel the weather.

Even a thick pelt couldn't fully protect a body from temperatures hovering around freezing.

Hot chocolate would do the trick, that and coffee. I could do other stuff, too, I reckoned. Get some breakfast started, for one. Libby and Elijah kept a freezer full of meat and a pantry full of canned goods and staples. Biscuits was a safe bet. Bacon and sausage, or country ham, if they was any stashed away somewhere. Eggs if anybody wanted some. Applesauce, which I knowed darn good and well Libby had on hand 'cause little Charlie ate the stuff like apples was going the way of the dodo.

I put on a fresh pot of coffee, then opened the fridge and poked my head in, trying hard to ignore the murmurs drifting to me from the living room and the insistent pull of my own second nature to join 'em. Lessee. There was a full pack of unsalted butter, a nearly full gallon of milk. I bet three growing boys really plowed through that. Jars of strawberry jam and what looked like grape or maybe blackberry jelly in the door, both about half full.

Yup, biscuits it was. I checked the time on my phone, sighed, and stuck it in the back pocket of my jeans. Not even six bells, still a good hour and a half before the sun even thought about waking the day up.

But I couldn't just go back out there and sit neither, not with guilt weighing so heavy in my heart.

All my fault.

It took ever ounce of my strength not to slam the refrigerator door shut. I took my energy out on the pantry instead, hunting down flour and lard from among the neat rows of goods lining the shelves. I had just set those on the kitchen counter and was about to root through drawers for a rolling pin when Riley strolled into the kitchen and stopped just inside the door.

"Hey, baby," he said. "Libby wondered where you'd gotten off to."

I turned my back on him and resumed my search. The guilt weren't something I wanted to talk on again and I didn't know how to explain the restlessness or the thin thread tying me to my daddy's clan, or my need to be doing something, anything, 'til we could figure out the best way to get Wyatt and them other young'uns back.

"Thought I'd whip up some biscuits," I finally said.

"You just need to be doing something." His voice was a tad dry and smudged with humor. "I would offer to help, but I'd rather not be whacked with that rolling pin."

I shot a narrowed eye glare at him over my shoulder, then plunked said rolling pin onto the counter beside the flour. "You keep that up and you'll go hungry."

He was quiet for a minute while I pulled out a bowl and started dumping flour into it, though I sworn, I could about feel his eyes boring into my back. Finally, he said, "I'm calling Dad in the morning and letting him know what's going on. He'll want to be in on it."

I shrugged. Sheriff Treadwell had as good a reason as any of us to want to figure out what was going on, the whos and whats and such, and he was mighty handy when it come to firearms. What use that'd be against magic, I had no ken. I never been up against a magic user before, not once, but the way I figured it, it never hurt to cover all the bases.

Speaking of.

"I reckon I better call in Missy, too," I said.

"Missy? What for?"

"Because she's a witch."

You coulda heard a pin drop behind me, Riley was so shocked. "Holy shit," he murmured.

"Yup, that about sums it up." I tapped the toe of my boot real gentle against the cabinet to my right. "Hunt me up a sheet pan, wouldja? I'm gonna need it in a minute."

Riley's hiking boots thudded against the linoleum as he walked toward me. Instead of hunting through the cabinets like I asked, he stopped right behind me, so close his body heat warmed my backside from shoulder to butt, and rubbed his chin against the top of my head. "This isn't your fault."

My hands paused in the middle of scooping lard into the flour.

"Don't deny it," he said. "Not when you've already told me so."

"Riley, I—"

He rested his hands on my hips and squeezed, shutting me up mighty quick. "Did I ever tell you why I left the military?"

His mama's visit to his roost sprung directly to mind. She told me things about Riley I was sure he'd never wanted me to know. I couldn't rightly confess to knowing it now, could I?

"No," I said. "I always wondered why, but I didn't want to poke my nose in."

"It's not poking, honey." The words was gentle, soft. He pressed a kiss to the top of my head. "I was in the hospital having my hip and leg reconstructed. Well, you know a lot of that."

I hummed under my breath. Yeah, I did know about that. I seen the scars for myself, hadn't I? Rubbed his leg when the muscles cramped up, took care of him when the medicine he took for them old injuries knocked him on his butt.

He sighed and relaxed behind me, leaning into me ever so slightly. "They finally moved me to a hospital in Atlanta, when I got well enough to be moved. Mama came to visit as often as she could. One day she came in and told me about Henry being missing, and a few days after that, she told me he was presumed dead."

My eyelids slid closed and my own wounds throbbed and ached in my chest. Henry gone because I'd trusted the deep wood. My baby was dead because of me.

"And as I lay there, helpless to do anything, I realized that if I hadn't gone into the Army, if I'd stayed here and been the same kind of friend to you as you'd been to me, then he'd still be with us."

That got my attention real quick. My eyes popped open and I turned in his arms, floured hands and all. "Now you listen here, Riley Treadwell. You ain't to blame for Henry dying."

"Yes, I am, Sunny." His expression was hard as stone, carved outta whatever emotion he'd pulled outta his heart. "I should've been here for him, and for you. If I had, you wouldn't feel like you had to chase down every goddamn, mischief making monster you run up against."

149

My temper flared hot. "I'da done that anyhow."

"No," he said flatly, though his eyes was gold in his anger. "If Henry hadn't died, you never would've gotten mixed up in that. We would've had a good life, Sunshine, a normal life, and I would've made damn sure neither one of you ever had to be in harm's way."

His words painted a perfect picture to me, of the love me and Henry missed out on all those years ago, of the family we coulda been if Riley hadn't been so cussedly stubborn, nor me neither, for that matter.

If was a powerful word. It conjured up all sorts of dreams and hopes and longings, but *if* weren't reality, and the reality was, Henry was dead. He was dead because of my lapse in judgment, not because Riley hadn't been here to protect him. I had to live with that guilt for the rest of my days, just like I had to live with the guilt of putting Libby's boys and, shoot, the entire Panther Clan at risk.

But that was my guilt, not Riley's, and I weren't gonna let him take the blame when the blame fell elsewhere.

I opened my mouth to tell him just that when his phone rung, startling us both.

He dug it outta his back pocket and answered it without breaking the hold his gaze had on mine. "Hello?"

"We've got a situation," Sheriff Treadwell said, just loud enough for me to hear it. "Where's Sunshine?"

"Right here." Riley pulled the phone away from his ear and clicked the speakerphone on. "Go ahead."

"Nora Vargas just showed up at my office." The cellphone crackled a bit, like the sheriff was shuffling paper around or going through a tunnel. "She's scared and hurt and asking for refuge."

"What happened?" I asked.

"She won't say," the sheriff said. "But she was clear on two points. First, she knows another child was taken."

"Wyatt Squirrel," Riley said. "One of Sunny's cousins."

"Jesus," the sheriff said on a near whisper. "That explains

the second point. She won't talk to anyone but Sunshine."

Relief filled me. No idea why. Maybe because Nora showing up outta the blue give me something constructive to do besides pound flour and lard into bread. Maybe because Nora would have answers to some of the questions plaguing me. Whatever the case, me and Riley needed to get there soon as we could.

I nodded at him, and he said, "We're on our way."

The sheriff said a curt goodbye and hung up, and Riley tucked his phone away. "I'll let Elijah and Libby know."

I turned around and snagged a dish towel off the counter. "Send somebody back to finish up the biscuits."

"You and your biscuits."

He brushed a kiss across my cheek and walked outta the kitchen, and I stuck my hands under the faucet, so grateful for the distraction Nora provided, I coulda kissed her.

THE SUN finally popped up during the drive from Libby's to the Sheriff's Department in Clayton, located in the bottom of the courthouse where the old jail used to be before the county built a fancy new detention center south of there in Tiger.

The Sheriff's Department was full of the kind of memories I'd rather not hold onto, what with it being the scene of so much family drama. Was here, back when it was a jail, that Sheriff Treadwell brung Mama when she killed my daddy. Fame done a short spell here, too, though now that I knowed what I did about the bad blood between him and the sheriff, I had to wonder if he weren't throwed in the pokey more outta spite than crime.

Fact was, I coulda recited another dozen or so kinfolk what'd gotten three hots and a cot in them very rooms, but I had more pressing concerns on my mind, like what Miss Nora Vargas was doing there.

We met Deputy Franks coming outta Sheriff Treadwell's office as we was going in. Todd was an old school chum of

Riley's. They played basketball together back in the day, Riley as a forward, Todd as the point guard. Now, if I recalled correctly, and I usually did, Todd had pretty good ballhandling skills. Him and Riley and t'others on the team done a fair number on other teams in the region.

But it weren't Deputy Franks' ballhandling skills I remembered him for. It was his freckles. God love him, but Todd had more freckles than any other human I ever seen and seemed to grow more ever day.

The other thing about Todd? He was friendly as a lap dog what'd just got a treat. Normally he smiled and waved and chitchatted, especially with Riley as they was still big buds.

Today, though, Deputy Franks nodded solemnly at us and passed right by without making so much as a peep. He held a little machine in his hands, one of them fancy pieces of techno crap used for scanning fingerprints, and that set me to wondering again.

I tucked my wonderings away and murmured hello to him, then stepped into the sheriff's office behind Riley. I been there before, not too long back as a matter of fact, soon enough to dismiss the furnishings without really looking on 'em. The sheriff sat behind his desk, which even now was tidy and neat as a pin, and in front of it in a fake leather chair sat Nora.

She didn't bother to look around when I shut the door, and soon as I was in good, I seen why. Her rich blonde hair was windblown and ratty, like she been pulled through a knothole backwards, and she was holding an ice pack to her jaw over a bruise blooming there. Her sweater and jeans looked not much the worse for wear, save for some dirt on her knees, but she was holding a scraped hand over her ribs and her breathing weren't quite even.

Riley held out the chair matching hers for me and I plopped into it next to Nora, ignoring the gentle warming of the ring through my shirt.

The sheriff was rolling a fancy ballpoint pen between the

fingers of both hands and his cold gaze was fixed on her. "Ms. Vargas is being held for questioning in the kidnappings of a dozen children."

"If she done it," I snapped, "I hardly think she'd show up here."

Riley put a restraining hand on my shoulder and murmured, "Sunny."

"Well, it wouldn't be the first time he went after the wrong body."

Sheriff Treadwell's head popped around to me. "If you want to be here while I question her, you'd better sit down and shut up."

I opened my mouth to spit out another retort, but Nora beat me to the punch.

"Stay," she said, her voice so soft, it was nearly lost in the anger whirling to life inside me.

"Spit it out then." Riley's hand tightened on my shoulder, a silent warning. I reined in the mad and blew it out in one long gust of air. "What happened?"

"I dug a little too deeply." Nora's laugh was bitter. She wiped a trembling hand over her face, then her eyes met mine. "When you dropped by Four Corners—"

Sheriff Treadwell's frown turned into a glare. "You went to the nature camp without me?"

"I sure did," I said, cheerful like. "Case you missed it, I'm a big girl now. Why, I can tie my shoes all by myself and ever thing, just like a regular grown up."

Riley's sigh held a hint of laughter. "You're not helping anything, Sunny."

I twisted around in my chair and looked way up at him. "Well, neither is he."

"Please," Nora said. "Time is running out. We only have until the cusp of the new moon."

"I knowed it," I muttered and turned back around, matching the sheriff's glare with one of my own. "Thirteen young'uns, right?"

I caught Nora's surprised expression out of the corner of my eye. "Yes, exactly. She needs thirteen children to complete the ritual."

"She?" Sheriff Treadwell said.

"Brenyn, one of the women in my coven." Nora laughed again, but it sounded less bitter than tired. "When Sunshine came by, I caught a fleeting glimpse of Brenyn's true nature, just as you were walking out."

"She caught a glimpse of my nature," I said. "I reckon that's why she come after the Panther Clan."

"A two-natured child. They hold such great power, that of beast and man." Nora shook her head and her eyelids slid shut on a grimace. "A woman like Brenyn couldn't resist the lure, doubly so if she knew it would hurt you. Very few question her and live."

"You did," the sheriff said.

"Yes," Nora said simply. "Not without help. Brenyn is quite old and very powerful."

"How old exactly?"

"Centuries. Her mother was the sorceress Carman, who died roughly a millennia and a half ago."

The name rung a bell, though it took me a minute to place it. Finally, some of the research I done popped into my head. "From Athens by way of Ireland."

Nora's eyelids popped open. "You know of her?"

"Wikipedia knows all."

"Smart ass," Riley said. "What I don't understand is why you didn't tell Dad and Sunny this from the beginning."

"I only just found out. After Sunny left and I caught the barest glimpse of Brenyn's true nature, I began searching through our archives. We have an excellent cataloging system, so it only took me a few minutes to find what I was looking for."

"And what was that?" I prompted.

"Nothing. There was no record of Brenyn in our system."

The sheriff tapped the end of his pen against the desk calendar spread out across the top of his desk. "And that's unusual because?"

Nora shrugged. "We keep a record of every witch or warlock we encounter, especially those within our coven."

"Then how did you find out about her?" I asked.

"I started digging."

"And dug too deep." I shook my head and relaxed against the back of my seat, and Riley. "But that ain't what sent you running to us."

"No," she said. "After I figured out who and what she was, it didn't take long to put two and two together and come up with a longevity ritual. Contrary to what mundanes believe, witches are not immortal."

"Mundanes?" the sheriff said.

"Non-magical humans." Nora's eyes slid to me and her mouth quirked into a half-grin. "And humans who are unaware of their own magic."

My eyebrows snapped down into a frown. I'd only just learnt about my own magical heritage a few months back. It was still a sore spot, rubbed plumb raw by knowing my daddy hid it from me and my grandma killed my boy over it.

Weren't nothing so sacred it was worth killing over.

The sheriff tapped his pen against the calendar again. "Describe this ritual to me."

"Death magic. It's the only way to extend one's life."

"That doesn't tell me anything."

Nora leaned forward in her chair, her eyes suddenly hard. "Thirteen souls must die a horrible, violent death under the dark of the moon."

"Ok," Sheriff Treadwell said kindly slow. "That can't be all there is to it."

"No, of course not." Nora shook her head and winced again. She touched the fingertips of her free hand to her forehead, rubbed a bit, then continued. "She needs twelve other witches or warlocks, some rare and deadly herbs, and a sacred, untainted oak grove."

"Let me guess," I said. "Y'all got them herbs already stored up."

"Of course. We keep a fully stocked Apotheke on site."

"I bet you have a sacred oak grove there, too," Riley said. The sheriff grunted. "Convenient."

Nora fairly bristled under his censure. "One of our primary duties is the protection of our natural habitat."

I reached over and placed a hand on her shoulder. "Settle down. We's just trying to get to the bottom of all this so's to retrieve them young'uns before Brenyn does 'em any more harm."

"Retrieve..." Nora slumped back into her chair and the blood drained from her face. "She'll kill you."

"She sure can try. Fact is, she's got my boy's half-sister and one of my cousins, and I ain't letting her keep neither one."

Nora swallowed, inhaled real slow, and when she spoke again, a quiet conviction underscored her words. "I understand, but you can't go in there alone. You'll need my magic, what's left of it after she tried to drain it, and you'll need more than these two men as backup."

I grinned at her. "Got a whole clan of two-natured what's ready to claw Brenyn open and eat her guts for dessert."

"That is perfectly gruesome," she said. "Thank Hecate for vegetarianism."

"Don't you worry none. We'll cure that problem for you." I leaned forward and fished my phone outta the back pocket of my jeans. "Got an ace up my sleeve, too, somebody what knows a thing or two about magic."

Sheriff Treadwell's eyebrows shot up. "You know a witch?"

"Oh, yeah. Couple of 'em, but one in particular." Phone in hand, I stood and nodded toward the door. "Be right back. Don't say nothing important while I'm gone."

Riley's hand slid off my shoulder as he grinned. "God

forbid you miss something."

The sheriff mumbled something under his breath, but I just went right on trucking out the door into the hallway. Some fights was worth picking and some wasn't. I liked to think I was old enough to know the difference.

17

Missy answered on the first ring and sounded like she was expecting my call. I explained what was going on as quick as I could while I paced up and down the hallway, not caring who heard me. Thing is, I was getting plumb tired of skulking around in the shadows, like they didn't exist. They was bad things in the world. What was the point in hiding 'em?

She was more'n happy to help Miss Nora out, though she refused to set foot in the Sheriff's Department. I told her I'd do what I could, then hung up and marched back into Sheriff Treadwell's office loaded for bear.

"Me and Riley is taking Nora with us," I said, right in the middle of whatever they was saying.

"We can all go," the sheriff said, surprising me good. I thought he'd argue more. Nope! He stood up, opened a drawer in his desk, and pulled out a pair of metal handcuffs. "She's wearing these."

I shook my head, intending to protest, but Riley was way ahead of me.

"C'mon, Dad," he said. "Is that really necessary?"

My grin was wide and mean. "Sure, it is. The good sheriff here is full of spite when he's of a mind."

Sheriff Treadwell narrowed a cold look on me, then calmly opened the drawer and laid the handcuffs back inside, so gentle, they didn't even chink together. "Where are we going?"

"Fame's," I said, so cheerful of a sudden, I coulda burst. Who'da thunk this whole mess woulda been enough to put the sheriff in his place? "Still wanna tag along?"

He nodded stiffly and pulled a holstered handgun out of the same desk drawer. "Let's go."

Riley shook his head, though he had sense enough not to utter word one. We waited while the sheriff and Nora pulled on winter jackets, then headed out to our vehicles, me and Riley in his Range Rover, the sheriff and Nora in his truck. The sun was full up now, though weak as a mewling babe. Clouds thinned out across the horizon and the bite of ice touched the air.

Snow soon, 'less I was mistaken. Maybe even today.

I nodded off not long after my butt hit the seat, and woke as we bumped up Fame's rutted driveway. Riley parked beside Fame's truck, in the spot where Trey usually parked, and the sheriff pulled in beside him. We all piled out and headed toward the trailer.

Missy opened the door before the first one of us put a foot on the steps leading up to it. She looked at us one by one, lingering on Nora for a bit, then her violet eyes turned cold as the winter wind. "You will behave, Chip Treadwell, or I will cast you out myself."

"Yes, ma'am," he said.

I swung around and looked at him good, but he was dead serious, though I coulda sworn I heard a trace of humor in his words.

Nora was standing stock still right beside him, her eyes as wide as saucers. "You're...ancient."

Missy's gaze landed on him and her sable curls shifted around her head, though not a trace of a breeze nudged the air. "Yes," she said, plain and simple. "Come inside before you catch cold."

We tromped in behind her one by one, first me and Riley, then Nora, and the sheriff in the rear. A fire burned in the wood stove, radiating heat. The meaty scent of bacon and fresh-made biscuits filled the air. Right on cue, my stomach remembered the breakfast I started at Libby's and grumped out a firm protest.

Fame was standing by the couch when we come in, hovering near where Gentry sat with Hob perched on his shoulder, both of 'em looking scared as spit.

Not Fame. He stiffened when the sheriff come in and his shooting hand twitched toward his waist, where he carried a gun when he was out taking care of his extralegal enterprises.

The sheriff nodded toward Fame, then doffed his hat. "This won't take long."

"It will take," Missy said, each word short and careful, "as long as it takes. Please. Have a seat. I've made breakfast."

I shrugged off my jacket and hung it by the door. "Thank you, Missy. I'm starving, but we got us a hurt witch here. I reckon she needs took care of before we eat."

"Mary Alice is on the way."

That give me pause. "Old Mother?"

"Trey's bringing her. She's a healer and a seer. I thought she should be here." Missy drew in a sharp breath. "We've time to eat, and while we're eating, you can share the details of how this young woman came to be among you."

Nora stepped forward and bowed her head respectfully. "Thank you, sister, for your kindness."

Missy nodded. "You've been badly wounded."

My stomach rumbled again. I placed a hand over it and tried real hard not to look as sheepish as I felt. "Sorry. We been up most of the night."

"Go on in the kitchen and help yourself." Missy placed her arm around Nora's shoulders and led her past us toward her and Fame's bedroom and the master bath. "You'll want a warm shower first, yes? I'll fetch you some clean clothes."

"Who are you?" Nora said, as they walked away, but if Missy replied, it was too low for me to catch.

Fame jerked his chin at the kitchen, his gaze careful on the sheriff. "You'll want to take your fill before Trey gets back with his woman."

"Lord knows that boy can eat," I muttered.

Riley snickered under his breath. "Come on, Dad. I'll show you where everything is."

I let them go on ahead of me and waited 'til they was fully in the kitchen and out of earshot before I spoke. "Sorry, Fame. He insisted on tagging along."

"Don't worry about it," he said. "You keep your mind on getting them young'uns back."

"It's weighing heavy on me."

"I know."

Gentry piped up just then. "I wanna help fight this time."

Me and Fame exchanged a glance, then I crossed the living room and knelt in front of my baby cousin, though he weren't hardly a babe no more. "They's witches this time, honey. They ain't like normal folk. The magic'll kill you before you can catch your breath."

Gentry's gentle mouth twisted into a sulk. "Trey's gonna go."

"Me, too," Fame said in a tone I knowed better'n to argue with.

I sighed and clasped my cousin's hand. "You stay here and keep Hob outta trouble. That's just as important as what we're doing, ya hear?"

Gentry pondered that for a minute, and finally, his expression cleared and he nodded. "But I get dibs on Miss Nora."

I bit my lower lip, holding in a laugh. "I think she's gonna wanna have a say in that, Gent."

Fame's hand fell on my shoulder. "Eat now, Sunny. You'll need your strength."

I pushed myself into a stand as weariness washed over me. I was gonna need more'n food before the day was done, but for now, I'd make do with whatever Missy'd fixed for breakfast.

ABOUT THE TIME Trey walked in the front door and on into the kitchen holding an appropriately dressed Old Mother by the hand, Nora stepped outta the hallway wearing some of Trey's castoffs, wafting the warm scent of soapy fresh with her coming. Her eyes widened when she saw the newcomers and she murmured, "A cunning woman. This family is full of surprises."

I shrugged and forked the last of my biscuits and gravy into my mouth. We was an odd bunch, of a certainty. I never thought of us that way, though. To me, we was just a family, plain and simple. 'Course, that was before I started hunting monsters, got visited by a demigod, learnt I was part painter myself, and discovered the witch in the family.

And that weren't even counting Trey courting a seer.

It kindly made my family's criminal undertakings seem mundane.

We made introductions all around. Trey and Mary Alice fixed themselves plates, then took two of the folding chairs Fame'd brung in while Nora was in the shower. Fame retreated to the doorway between the kitchen and living room and leaned a shoulder against it, and Missy promptly moved her chair over to where he stood.

I scooted off my seat and held it out for Nora. "You want, I can fix you a plate. The gravy's made from bacon grease, so I reckon you don't want none of that."

"Waste not, want not," she said.

I eyed her over Riley's auburn head. "I thought you was a vegetarian."

She smiled faintly. "Bacon is my weakness."

Well, Lordy. We should all have such weaknesses.

I shook my head and dumped my plate in the sink for later clean up, then took down a clean plate and started piling food on it for Nora. The way I figured it, her body needed food to help heal what was ailing her, and by golly, a Southern kitchen was the best place to find healing food.

Missy spoke into the scrapings of forks on china. "What brings you here, Nora?"

"Brenyn." Nora folded her hands together in her lap and kept her gaze on me. "But you knew that already."

"I had my suspicions, and I warned Sunny to stay far away from her."

I turned right then, holding a plate full of food, and locked gazes with Nora. "What can I say? I never was one to listen to my elders."

Riley hid a snort of laughter behind a sip of milk, but Fame just shook his head. I grinned at my uncle and plopped Nora's plate and a fork down in front of her.

Sheriff Treadwell leaned back in his chair and rubbed his hands across his belly. "I still don't understand exactly what this Brenyn is up to."

"In a nutshell? Siphoning off the life forces of the young to extend her own life." Nora picked up the fork and poked at the gravy covered biscuit crumbles on her plate. "It's a grotesquely evil spell. Only the most wicked can cast it."

"Or the most determined," Missy said. "Something fuels her."

"Revenge." Ever eye in the place turned to me. I shrugged and leaned my butt against the kitchen counter, facing the folks gathered in the heart of Fame and Missy's home. "Brenyn's mama went head to head with the Tuatha Dé Danann when she tried to invade Ireland. They captured her instead and imprisoned her, and banished her sons."

Dread crept into Missy's expression and she sat straight up in her chair. "Brenyn's half-brothers. Are they here?"

Nora's mouth thinned and she set the fork down with a clatter. "One is that I know of. Dubh. He is...was..."

It took me a second to figure out why she was so hesitant, and when I did, you coulda knocked me over with a feather. "You was dating the son of an evil sorceress?"

"Well, I didn't know who he was at the time," she said, a mite defensive. "And we only went out a few times."

I snickered. "I bet that's out the window now."

Missy cut a reproving glance at me. "I've heard of Dubh. He's known as the Black."

"I always thought it was because he was dark headed." Nora shook her own golden locks. "But now? I'm guessing he'll be one of the twelve Brenyn calls on during her ritual."

Riley sat back in his chair, mirroring his daddy. "What I don't get is why Brenyn needs this ceremony, but they don't."

"Rumor has it," Missy said, "that Carman's sons were fathered by a god. It could be that they're immortal in their own right."

Nora shrugged. "Or it could be that they have their own ceremonies to extend their mortality."

I slapped my hands against the edge of the counter. "What I know is, all this talk ain't getting us where we need to be, which is figuring out how to bring Brenyn down and save them young'uns."

"We need to move quickly," the sheriff said.

"Tonight." The soft-spoken word silenced us all. Mary Alice's full mouth trembled into a smile. "I've seen it."

Trey draped an arm around her, his expression pinched with concern. "You promised me you wouldn't do that no more."

"Even I can't control the foretellings, Trey. They come, or they don't. The herbs?" She shrugged one shoulder and lowered her dark eyed gaze to her plate. "They only aid the process."

Missy stood and closed the short distance between herself and Old Mother, then knelt beside her and Trey. "What did you see, darling?"

Mary Alice squinched her eyes closed for a minute. A tremor run through her once, twice, and her eyes popped back open and rolled back in her head, showing nothing but white. "A red stain grows upon the land bearing Death, Evil, and Strife. Thirteen shall be the hand and thirteen the heart, and on the night of nights, the sickle shall reap the harvest."

A chill run down my spine and I shivered. It was the first time one of Old Mother's foretellings made any sense to me beforehand, and I didn't like how close it hit to the dream what'd come to me just last night.

Trey shook Mary Alice gently, but she was into it now, rocking back and forth against the table. I knowed from experience it was best to let the foretelling run its course, lest her hoodoo reached out and slapped you into next week.

It'd done that to me before. Weren't an experience I aimed to repeat.

"Black is the heart," she said in that rolling African lilt. "Red is the blood. Three shall be one and one shall be three."

"Baby," Trey said, and I shook my head. Weren't no stopping her now, no matter how bad he wanted to spare her.

Mary Alice continued like he hadn't said a word. "And the heir of the dead shall walk the night with the mother of the spirit, and death shall be no more."

She shuddered once and slumped against him, and when she lifted her head, she was my cousin's girlfriend again, not the seer what kept walking outta the woods and visiting prophecies on me.

Missy stood and smoothed a hand over Trey's dishwater blond hair. "Help her to your bed, darling. She needs rest."

Mary Alice shook her head and pushed herself upright. "No, I have work to do still." Her voice was blessedly normal, if scratched and hollow. "I need to do what I can to heal Nora and restore her magic to her."

"It can wait," Trey said.

Mary Alice just shook her head again. "It has to be done tonight, before Brenyn has a chance to begin her dark work."

"Half an hour," Missy said, "then you and Nora can retreat to your cabin."

Trey stood and looked down at Mary Alice, his mouth set in a firm line. "You go on in and lay down. I'll bring you some orange juice."

Sheriff Treadwell leaned forward in his chair. "If we're going in tonight, we need to know more. We need maps and weapons. We need a plan."

"Right," I said and pushed away from the counter. "We'll get to all that. First, I need to call Libby and give her the four one one."

A slow, wicked smile bloomed on Fame's face. "The good sheriff here don't know about your daddy's kin, does he, Sunny?"

I glanced at Riley, who shook his head once, then I grinned real big. "No, he does not."

Sheriff Treadwell glanced between the three of us. "What about your father's family?"

"Oh, you're gonna wanna see this'un for yourself," I said. Me, I couldn't wait to see how he reacted to a bunch of Cherokees getting buck nekkid and shifting into painters in front of God and ever body.

18

We went our separate ways half an hour later, once breakfast was cleared away and Trey let Mary Alice get up from her post-prophecy nap. Him and her led the sheriff and Nora away to Mary Alice's cabin. Me and Riley retired to my trailer down the hill, but not before I called Libby and told her the plan.

We was meeting at four o'clock that afternoon on the dot to make what preparations we could for the coming night.

I was so tired by the time we made it to the trailer, I stripped to my skin straight away and dropped into bed next to Riley. He curled around me under the covers, warming me the way he always done. Unselfishly, without reserve or hesitation.

I really should do better by him. I really should...

The alarm on Riley's phone burst into reveille, startling me out of a deep sleep, and I about jumped outta my skin.

"What in tarnation, Riley?" I yelped.

He reached across me and slapped around on my nightstand, his eyes closed tight as clams. By feel, he cut off the alarm and set his phone back down. "Five more minutes, babe."

"Tempting," I said and tried to roll outta bed.

His arm tightened around me. Next thing I knowed, I was flat on my back underneath him, his face was buried in my nape, and his manly parts was prodding at my womanly parts.

"Riley, honey."

My voice come out all breathy and weak, then he slipped into me and I didn't think another thought 'til well after them five minutes was up, the scoundrel.

THE THING about me and Riley is, I knowed what he was up to when he made love to me that afternoon. Now, not in the moment, no. He plumb took me outta body and soul then, sending me nigh on into Heaven.

But once I floated back to Earth, long about the time me and him piled into my shower for a quick wash off, I realized exactly why he chose that moment instead of waiting.

We was going into battle tonight together, facing God only knowed what. Chances was good we wasn't coming out the other side whole.

I wanted so bad to tell him he had to stay here with Gentry and Old Mother and Hob. I wanted to tell him I couldn't risk him dying, too, that it was ok if the Reaper took my soul, but I needed him to be safe. I needed him to be happy and whole and as well as a body could be, considering all he been through.

The words bottled themselves up behind my tongue, sticking in my throat. I sat on the bed watching him sort through the go bag he kept in the Range Rover, picking up this gun or that box of ammo, testing this knife or t'other 'til he was plumb satisfied with his weapons.

He was a trained soldier. That's what I kept telling myself, repeating the short sentence over and over again inside my mind with one hand resting over my heart and t'other in a white-knuckled grip in my lap. Riley was a trained soldier. He knowed one end of war from t'other. Sure, he was injured in the line of duty and still bore the scars, but he could handle himself in a fight.

He weren't scared of hardly nothing, see? And that's where my problem lay.

"They's gonna be magic," I said outta the blue. "In them woods. This ain't like Afghanistan."

He grunted and pulled back the slide of the 1911 he was holding, loading a round of ammunition, then checked the safety. "It's just like Afghanistan. People are people. They'll have weapons I may not understand, but I understand guerilla fighting. That's what we're facing tonight, Sunny, a bunch of people who know their territory and don't want us there."

His voice was flat, completely devoid of emotion, and so hard my heart thumped faster under my palm. "But it's magic and—"

"And nothing." He set the 1911 down and picked up a Glock 19. "I think this grip is small enough for your hand."

"I got my own dadgum guns, Riley Treadwell," I snapped. "And like as not, they won't do squat against whatever them witches is gonna throw at us."

He set the Glock down and finally looked at me. "Sunny, baby."

I stood up so fast, my feet hit the floor 'bout the same time my legs straightened out. "Don't you 'Sunny, baby' me. We don't know what we're walking into, and you act like you ain't got a care in the world."

"I've got a care, baby. I've got so many cares." He reached out and dragged me into a hug, holding me so tight I could scarce breathe. "But you can't think about that when you go into these situations. You have to think about the mission and your squadron. You have to do whatever it takes to stay alive, and if that means setting your emotions aside, then that's what you have to do."

I breathed him in, taking the scents of laundry detergent and soap clinging to him into me. My heart was a giant, throbbing lump of worry in my chest.

He was right. That didn't make it easier to hear.

Finally, he relaxed his hold, cupped my chin, and tilted my head up so our eyes met. "I know you're scared, baby. It's ok to be scared."

"I ain't scared for me, Riley." The words tumbled outta me, breaking down the dam what'd held 'em back. "I'm scared for you. If something happened to you—"

"Nothing is going to happen to me." He brushed his mouth across mine, then hugged me tight again. "I've got too much to live for."

I turned my face into his chest, hiding the tears threatening to spill over onto my cheeks. That was something me and him had in common, weren't it? We both had something to live for now, and like him, I was gonna do ever thing in my power to hold onto it with both hands. I done lost Daddy and Henry. Damned if I was gonna lose a single other soul in my life, starting with the man standing right in front of me.

BY THE TIME we walked up the hill to Fame's trailer, the parking lot was crowded with vehicles. Fame and Trey's, of course, but also the sheriff's truck, Libby's sedan, and a coupla others what seemed familiar.

The living room was jam packed full of folks, so many they overflowed into the kitchen. I picked out Mary Alice and Gentry and Riley's mama's voices coming from in there. Playing cards, was my guess. Whatever it took to keep Gentry occupied.

Though I was surprised the sheriff possessed the

wherewithal to bring his wife into the den of her ex-boyfriend, albeit one from her teenage years.

My daddy's daddy sat on the couch next to Libby and Elijah. Nora was squeezed in on t'other side and Missy perched on the sofa's arm next to her. Fame'd took a wide-legged stand behind her, though how he fit into the space was beyond me. The sheriff, Noel, and some other elders of the Panther Clan was ranged around the room sitting on whatever they could scrounge up.

My heart sank plumb to my knees. They wasn't enough of us here. Surely to God we'd need more'n this.

Libby smiled wanly at me. "We've got a busload more on the way."

I raised my eyebrows at her. "A busload?"

"They're meeting us in Helen."

Noel shifted on the folding chair he'd settled into and glanced up at me. "We can feel your worry, Sunny."

Well, that made two of us 'cause I was full of the stuff. I inhaled slowly, trying to rein it in, and felt it drain outta me like a plug was pulled. Oh, it was still there, but in the background where it didn't take up too much space.

Elijah leaned forward and poked a finger at the map spread out on the coffee table in front of him. "Now, these are the boundaries of the nature camp and here's the only entrance."

"That's right," Nora said. "They'll expect us there. I suspect someone has already booby-trapped the road in with some kind of dampening spell. We'll have to walk in on foot from there."

"And risk being ambushed." The sheriff leaned back in his chair and laced his fingers together behind his head. "The hollow widens after a quarter mile and the forest gets pretty thick."

"We can slip through the trees." Johnny rubbed his palms together and a wily smile cracked his wrinkled features. "We ain't confined to the road like you two-legged runts."

I slid my palm over my mouth, hiding a smile. The old coot was enjoying this a bit too much, you ask me, but at his age, I reckoned he could enjoy any dadgum thing he wanted.

Noel stared placidly at the map, not even a trace of humor in his expression. "They'll be expecting us to come in from all sides."

"Then they'll expect us," Elijah said, his voice flat. "Now, the way I see it, we need to break up into teams. Somebody has to find the kids while the rest of us take on the witches. Thirteen or so, is that right?"

"More," Nora murmured. "We're Wiccans. An' it do no harm. That's our primary drive, to never hurt others, to do only good."

Missy smoothed a hand over Nora's shoulder. "Not everyone has your pure heart."

"They'll stand with her, pure heart or not." Nora shook her head, though her hand crept across her body and up, and latched onto Missy's fingers, drawing comfort where she could, I reckoned. "We're too conditioned to banding together against outsiders for them not to. It won't matter what I say. I've already tried."

"I thought some of 'em helped you escape," I said.

"Only because they truly believe in doing no harm." A tear rolled down her cheek and she sniffed. "When it comes down to it, my sisters will always choose their own above all others."

If she was aware of the contradiction in her words, it didn't show, but I caught the slip and so did Missy. I could see it in her face. Nora's heart was divided. On the one hand, she still thought of the coven as her family; yet at the same time, she recognized that she'd become an *other* to them the minute she turned against Brenyn.

I almost felt sorry for her, woulda if I weren't well aware of the danger she posed to us all.

Time enough to deal with that. I'd make sure ever body knowed about the pull the coven still had on Nora, if they hadn't picked it up on their own.

I settled back against Riley, leaning into him while I could, and let the conversation wash over me. Something coiled restlessly inside me, tightening into a heady knot of anticipation. There was a battle ahead. Blood would be spilled, maybe some of my own, but the painter inside of me, that tiny instinct what'd been growing in my mind and soul these past few months, it didn't care. Blood was blood, and it was eager to paint its paws red.

19

Our convoy musta looked quite the sight going down the road. Half a dozen cars bracketed a white school activity bus borrowed from the Graham County public school system. Turns out one of my cousins up Libby's way drove the bus and the county's school superintendent owed her a favor.

Big favor, letting an employee drive county property into a witch fight. I reckoned the exact nature of the bus's use didn't get back to the superintendent, else he wouldn'ta lent it out.

We hit the turnoff for the nature camp just after sunset. About a quarter mile down the road, just outta sight of the main road, the school bus pulled onto a wide grassy spot along the shoulder and parked along with a couple of the cars. Nearly three dozen of my Cherokee kinfolk streamed outta the bus, men and women alike, nekkid as the day they was born. They slipped into the shadows of the woods where I imagined they found any old spot to transform.

Riley'd drove me, Fame, and Missy down. When I twisted 'round to watch my Cherokee kin go, making sure they was safe, he said, "Forget it, sweetheart. The only naked man you'll be seeing from now on is me."

Fame chuckled from the front passenger seat, but I just turned back around and frowned. Them was the strongest of my kin. The rest was back home with Johnny, guarding the children and them of the clan what was too weak to protect themselves.

Nearly three dozen painters, plus me and Riley, Fame and Missy, Trey, Sheriff Treadwell, and Nora. No matter how I tallied the numbers, it just didn't seem like enough.

Not half a mile from the lodge, the front vehicle, drove by the sheriff, petered out and sputtered to a stop in the middle of the road. He got out and waved to us as Riley slowed to a stop, then the Range Rover's engine coughed and knocked, and Riley braked hard.

"It just died," he muttered. "Goddamn it. I just had it looked over, too."

I was busy looking at the woods surrounding us. Now, I been down here a coupla times before, so I was familiar with the view.

That is, I was familiar with how the view was supposed to look. Tonight, in the last of the sunlight filtering over the mountaintops, where healthy trees once was now stood a dying wood steeped in fog and unnatural shadow.

The ring warmed against my chest, under my shirt.

"It's not the car, darling," Missy said as she unbuckled. She glanced around and her worried gaze met mine. "They know we're here."

That dampening spell Nora mentioned. Hang it all, it woulda been nice if she'da been wrong just this once.

I sucked in a long, slow breath and let it out the same way. Show time.

Nerves jittered inside of me like grasshoppers hopping around in my tummy. I opened the door, slid out into the chilly air, and shivered inside the fleecy jacket I borrowed from Anne. It was snug, but moved with my ever move. It was also thin enough for the wind to cut right through it. That was fine with me. I'd warm up soon enough.

Probably.

Riley dropped a kiss to the top of my head as he passed by me on the way to the weapons and flashlights stored in the rear of his SUV. I had my daddy's hunting knife strapped to my hip where I could reach it quick. No guns. Riley could keep his. I aimed to get up close and personal.

Besides which, me, Missy, Libby, and Nora was assigned kid duty. Nora insisted on it during our planning phase, something about there being strong magic in motherhood. She had no kids, Missy was pregnant, Libby had her three, and my boy was gone from this life.

Powerful magic, she said, and started in on an anecdote from the movie version of *The Witches of Eastwick*, but that'un went straight over my head.

A painter, its fur black as night, strolled up to me then and butted its head playful like against my thighs. I squatted down and rubbed behind its ears, murmuring hello to Libby.

The click of a gun cocking stopped me in mid rub. I glanced over my shoulder. There was the sheriff, his skin pasty under the First American Bank ball cap he wore. His hands was wrapped around a good old-fashioned revolver held low in front of him.

Riley come up beside him and nudged his daddy's hands away. "Don't shoot. She's with us."

I stood and didn't do a dadgum thing to hide the smirk growing on my mug. "T'other painters might take offense if you shoot one of their own."

Missy shot me a reproachful glance. "Don't shoot any of the panthers, Chip. Those are our Cherokee friends in their animal form."

"Animal..." Sheriff Treadwell gaped at me for a minute, then ever so slow, he holstered his gun. "I guess this is what it feels like to be pranked."

Riley clapped him on the shoulder. "That's the spirit, Dad."

Soon as we gathered together in a group, we left the cars and headed down the road toward the lodge, letting our flashlights sweep ahead of us in broad arcs. The forest closed in around us as the sunlight winked out and the sky overhead abruptly went from the deep, fiery pinks of sunset to the deepest black of a moonless night.

Leaves rattled along the forest floor as ghostly shades flitted from tree to tree. The painters was well ahead of us, surrounding the lodge. Whatever it was in the forest, I couldn't feel it, couldn't get a sense of it. My senses was dead, as a matter of fact, numbed by the nerves jumping in my stomach, or the fear clamping down on my heart, or the cold seeping through the thin layers of clothing I wore, or maybe all three.

The men ranged out ahead of us, each holding a gun of some sort along with a flashlight. Each of 'em was carrying extra ammo and probably other weapons as well. We women had decided to go in as we was, save for my knife and the zip ties Nora suggested we bring along. Libby had her claws, I had my knife and a whole lotta gumption. Missy's magic was strong, so Nora said, and once Old Mother recharged Nora's batteries, hers was, too, though she claimed her own talents was of a lesser degree to Missy's.

The plan was this: we four would find the young'uns, based on Nora's knowledge of the camp and Brenyn's plans, and ever body else was to draw the witches away.

Sounded simple enough, right? Only it didn't feel so simple in the doing.

A painter screamed in the distance. Libby's ears twitched forward and her long tail swished, but she stayed right where she was, walking between me and the woods, her steps much quieter'n ours. Something moaned beyond her, an owl hooted behind us, and my skin began to crawl.

Something, or somebody, was watching us.

I shook off the urge to rub a hand over my nape. Instead, I reached across my torso and drawed Daddy's knife from the sheath at my waist. The hilt was firm in my hand, hard, and the sharpened curve of its edge seemed to glow all on its own.

Nonsense, of course. It was just a knife.

Just as the lodge come into view, a painter roared, then a woman screamed, and all around us, people streamed outta the woods, dozens and dozens of 'em, all dressed in black. Their hands wove in and around, gathering light and heat, drawing magic from the air or the woods or another dimension, for all I knowed.

One woman throwed her hands at us, pushing out a ball of light. Missy shoved me forward as she stepped back, and the light zinged overhead, scorching hot, just missing our heads. The smell of burnt hair floated around me, but I didn't have time to worry on it. One minute the eight of us was together in our little clump, and the next we scattered, each charging toward the witches and warlocks bearing down on us in the night.

IT WAS a free for all. I lost track of who was doing what and concentrated on fighting my way to the lodge, where we was gonna look for the young'uns first. A woman I vaguely recognized swiped a glowing hand at me. I brushed it aside and jabbed at her mouth, bam, bam, making contact each time, dropping my flashlight in the process. Her head popped back and blood gushed outta her nose, and the barest hint of pain radiated away from my knuckles into my hand.

As I was reaching for her to put her down on the ground for the count, somebody pulled my ponytail, yanking my own head back. I hissed out a breath, swung my elbow back high, and connected with an arm, then stabbed my foot back, hoping to hit shins.

Missed.

I caught a wide, sweeping motion outta the corner of my eye just as Nora slung a transparent disc in front of me, blocking a ball of lightning aimed straight at my gut, bouncing it into the woods where it hit a magic-blackened tree and lit it on fire.

And that's about when I decided enough was enough.

I reached back and grabbed the top of my ponytail tight in my fist, then jerked my head forward, bringing my hapless attacker along with me. He or she (or it, for all I knowed) stumbled into me, knocking me forward, and in the process, they let go of my hair. I whirled around swinging my knife hilt first and connected with the cheekbone of the man I seen jogging when me and the sheriff was here.

His head whipped around and back again, like he was used to being punched, and he spat blood outta his mouth. "Bitch."

I let some of my mama's crazy bleed into my feral grin and kicked his feet out from under him. Down he went, flat on his back. The breath whooshed outta him, but more fool him, he tried to roll over on his side, like he was gonna get up.

Nunh-unh.

I dropped down on top of his legs, drawed my fist back, and punched him square in the jaw, knocking him out cold. His head lolled to the side and he went limp, just as I intended. I scooted off him around the melee of legs and feet scurrying around us, rolled him over, and zip tied his hands behind his back.

One down, a few dozen to go.

All around me, chaos reigned. Flashlights rolled along the ground, their cones of light illuminating random patches of fighting and, beyond that, the eerie forest surrounding us. A coupla other trees was on fire, their light casting flickering shadows where the flashlights missed. Not a single shot had been fired, though knives aplenty glinted in the erratically lit space.

Lights of all colors flashed around us, looking for all the world like dud fireworks, but not all the magic was flashes and booms of light. Ahead of me, near the lodge, a red-headed witch flicked her fingers at a painter. It reared upright onto its hind legs and flipped over on its back, twitching in the shadows at the edge of the light's reach.

I rolled back onto my haunches and was about to launch myself in that direction when a firm hand pressed me down. Another ball of light screamed by us, going about where my head woulda been if I'da stood up. I glanced around. Riley was squatting behind me, his expression grim as death.

"Watch the sky, baby," he said, then he twisted around and launched himself at the two women Missy was fending off.

Ozone drifted through the air, mingling with the humid bite of cold fog. A by-product of the magic, I figured. Behind me, a painter yowled. I glanced around and up, making sure nothing was coming at me, then turned and headed in the direction of the downed painter, just in time to see another painter casually swipe a clawed paw at the red-headed witch.

She looked down, both hands held to her stomach. In what little light gathered around her, blood glinted red as it oozed between her fingers. She dropped to her knees and onto her side, like a marionette with cut strings, and the painter turned and just as casually trotted toward its downed kin.

And that's when I saw it, a clear-cut path straight to the lodge.

I launched myself into a run, straight toward it, ducking flying elbows and fists and the occasional ball of magic amidst grunts and groans and the scuffling of feet on asphalt. To my left, the sheriff fell to a knee. I veered off and pulled a warlock off of him, then together, me and the sheriff wrestled the man to the ground and zip tied him.

"Pray none of them get hold of a knife," he muttered to me, and I nodded and went back at it.

Libby fell in beside me as I run. I knowed her by feel more'n looks. To me, the painters was nearly alike save for their size or gaits. Couldn't tell 'em apart by looks as they all had coal black fur and them unnatural green eyes, but the feel of 'em was different.

I rolled that nugget around in my mind for a minute, then tucked it away for later thought.

A painter tackled the witch Nora was fighting as we passed, and she broke off and joined us, then a tingle run down my spine and I knowed Missy was there, jogging with us. My hand found Libby's head and slid down to her ruff. I twisted my fingers into the hair growing there as Nora's hand clapped over mine and Missy's over hers.

It was like ever thing locked into place then, four pieces of a puzzle only we could make.

A blast wave radiated away from us, blowing a hard wind. The fighting paused as the wind whipped over the beings gathered there and they all turned to us, looking on the magic we wrought.

I didn't understand it. I mean, yeah, Nora'd explained it to me, but I hadn't really understood 'til now.

There was power in the balance, power in the different stages of motherhood we represented, power in the way we come together. Mother potential, mother awaiting, mother in the now, mother mourning. What could ever be more powerful than parents united for the sake of children?

Ahead of us, the lodge's double doors opened, and out come Brenyn in all her glory, dressed in a flowing black dress. She stepped gracefully onto the rock landing on top of the stairs leading into the lodge. Even from here in the uncertain light I could make out the sharp glint of her smile.

"Melissa." Her voice was a purring coo spoken into the silence left behind by the blast wave. "It was kind of you to join us."

Missy's hand locked tight on ours, the only sign of her nerves, if she was nervous a'tall. When she spoke, her voice

181

was strong and sure, and rang through the night as clear as a bell. "Where are the children, Brenyn? Give them to us and you may yet survive this night."

Brenyn throwed back her head and laughed. Behind her, two men bled outta the shadows, like they was a part of it. Nora hissed in a breath, and that was all I needed to identify 'em as two of Brenyn's half-brothers.

Brenyn's laughter stopped abruptly and her smile fell from her face. "The children are mine. Their life forces, their souls, their energy. They will be sacrificed so that I and my brothers may face the immortal bastards who killed our mother."

Low murmurs drifted to us, broken by the occasional word, and finally, somebody shouted, "You never told us the children would die."

Nora glanced at me beneath half-shuttered eyelids, then she lifted her head and spoke. "Sisters and brethren, Brenyn has mislead you all. She is an ancient sorceress, the daughter of Carman, a reviled warrior and enchantress."

"Lies," somebody hissed. A painter growled deep in its throat and a human yelped.

I was guessing somebody got swiped at none too gentle by the wrong end of a paw.

"She's telling the truth," Missy said. "You can feel it in your hearts, and if you can't feel it, then believe me. Brenyn is using you."

"Who are you to interfere?" a man called.

Missy drawed in a deep breath and let it out again, and with it, the power she been holding back long as I knowed her come out, too. Gasps rose around us and painters shifted uneasily, but Missy weren't done yet.

"I am Melissa," she said, imbuing magic into each word. "An enchantress of old and the companion of Merlin, who has long since passed from this Earth."

In my mind, a tiny voice started rising in me, and the ring went from a steady heat to scorching hot, nigh on burning me.

Use the ring, this'un whispered. *Use it now.*

I tightened my free hand around the hilt of Daddy's knife, fighting the temptation to shake my head or tug at my earlobe as an argument broke out around us. Couldn't hear what was being said over that instinct clawing at me louder and louder, egged on by some unknown force outside of me, but I got the gist.

Something wanted me to use the ring, only I didn't have a dadgum clue how I was supposed to do that.

The arguing escalated and them glowy hands popped back up. The coven was splitting in two. The fight was about to break out again, only now, weren't no way to tell who was friend and who was foe. We had to act quick if we wanted to rescue them young'uns. We had to get past Brenyn and her brothers before the witches and warlocks around us chose sides.

Nora was speaking now, yelling into the escalating argument. A hand brushed over my hair and Missy whispered in my ear, "Put the ring on, darling."

I shook my head, trying to sort out what she was saying from the growing urgency of my own instinct. "You told me—" I swallowed hard and tried again. "You told me to never put it on."

"Because I wasn't sure what it would do."

"I don't know what to do." The words popped outta me before I could stop 'em. "It'll make me invisible, right? I can slip past Brenyn and search the lodge while y'all hold 'em off."

"It might." Her breath blew against my ear, then she whispered even softer, "Or it might draw on the power you already possess and do something entirely different."

Light exploded into the night and Nora staggered away from us. Her hand slipped outta the hold we had and whatever magic we'd conjured snapped in two.

Instinct took ahold of me. I ducked down and wrapped myself around Libby's head, protecting her as the fight broke out around us. Missy skirted us and run straight toward Brenyn, throwing spells at her as she went, judging by the way her hands flicked and curved.

"Use the ring," she screamed at me, and that was the last straw on my back.

I shoved Daddy's knife into its sheath, yanked the ring outta my shirt, breaking the chain holding it around my neck, and shoved it onto the pointing finger of my left hand. Fire burst to life inside me, exploding outward. I flung my arms out and lifted my face to the dark moon hanging above us, and screamed as pain suffused me from skin to bone and ever where in between.

20

Libby backed away from me, nice and easy, her gaze never leaving me as I panted through the pain gripping me. A thread thinned between us, strengthened, waned again, and from somewhere far off, dozens of hushed voices whispered in my mind.

My stomach twisted into knots and my joints popped. I glanced down at my hands and gasped. They was gnarled and twisted, broken almost, and the skin writhed and squirmed, like something crawled underneath, just outta sight.

Through the noise of the resurrected fight, a gruff, gravelly voice said, "What's...happening..."

Me, that was. My voice. I clawed at my throat, felt something rip through my skin. Libby leapt forward, bit down on my forearm, and yanked my hand down, away from my jugular.

Accept it. Her voice now, echoing to me from so far

away, but there in my mind. *Embrace the pain, Sunshine.*

My arm in her mouth. My gaze was drawn there, to the gentle bite of sharp teeth, to the skin fighting against itself.

Energy built inside me, straining for release. I clamped my eyes shut, trying to hold it in as my fingers flexed against the unnatural pain gripping me. Couldn't give in. Couldn't let go. Couldn't...

Accept it, another voice said in my mind, deeper now, familiar, tugging at something I long thought lost.

My eyes popped open as I searched through memory, frantic to place that voice, that sweet, sweet voice...

"Daddy!" I said. Tears popped into my eyes, unbidden, and my heart constricted around the joy bursting through me. "Daddy! Where are you?"

Here, Sunny. I been here all along.

His voice drifted in and outta focus, in and outta volume, like my brain was tuning to a radio frequency only I could hear.

Don't fight it, baby. Don't fight...

Then his voice was gone, drowned by a thousand voices clamoring for attention in my head. The dissonance shot through me, ratcheting the pain to a level so high, I thought I was gonna die from it. I gritted my teeth as they roared at me, and finally, one by one, their words resonated together into a fragmented song.

Don't...fight...join...us...be...free...

My head rolled back and I stared up at the moonless sky, at the million million pinpricks of light gazing back at me, and I accepted the truth of what I was and let that energy go.

And embraced the release of it into the night.

Fur black as midnight popped outta my skin, bones twisted me from human to other.

I dropped to all fours and stared at the satisfied expression gracing Libby's painter face. Satisfied, gratified, pleased. The twin of her emotion fluttered into my mind.

No, not my mind. My soul.

The pain eased and dissipated as my two halves joined, my human self, that part of me I always knowed, and the painter part, that part of me what was so small, I never woulda knowed it was there if not for Libby. I arched my back, grateful for the pain's passing, and felt muscles and ligaments stretch, accommodating my new structure. My tongue rolled outta my mouth, sliding against sharp canines, and I purred.

Dear sweet Jesus, it felt heavenly.

The energy throbbed one last, sharp time, and I inhaled against the final stab of pain and glanced around.

The night was clear to me, as if the sun had crested the horizon and hung there, shedding its light into a new day. It was more than that, though. Things were crisper now, clearer. I saw more, heard more, *felt* more, though I couldn't discern how or what, or even why.

Libby batted a paw at me, drawing my attention back to her, but for the life of me, all I could think on was how good it felt to be a painter.

And how good it felt to finally be whole.

SOON AS she got my attention, Libby twisted around and leapt toward the lodge. I writhed free of my clothes and took off after her, stumbling like a newborn colt on my newborn legs. Missy had doubled back and was running beside me, her hands a vicious swirl in the air as she shot off round after round of her magic at Brenyn, and defended us both from the same.

Nora was behind us, edging slowly back as she defended our rear. I could feel her, feel the magic flowing in and outta her the same way I heard my daddy and Libby in my mind.

They was a part of me, and now, so was Nora.

I got it all wrong. The mother magic didn't break when our hands fell apart. It was still there, binding us together. I couldn't feel it before I put the ring on, but now? Now, I could trace the patterns the same way I traced letters for

Henry when he was learning his ABCs. The shape of the magic, the taste of it, the sound and glory, the knowledge flowed into me, filling me from stem to stern, and I wallowed in it.

They was more there, too, a deeper connection throbbing to life, something familiar and bone deep and new all at once, something ancient and wise. A recognition, a belonging, like a door opened, one I never seen before, but through it was the home what was meant just for me and mine.

It was tempting to stop and figure it all out. For dang sure, I wanted to. I had a job to do tonight, an important one, and I weren't gonna let my curiosity stand in the way of them young'uns' freedom.

My legs steadied a mite the more I used 'em. Up ahead, Libby bounced up the rock stairs and landed smack dab against one of the brothers, knocking him flat on his back. I heard his breath whoosh outta his lungs from all the way over here and grinned a very painter like smile.

What goes around comes around.

Missy broke off and swung around me, and I slipped past Brenyn and the other brother, though for the life of me not 'cause of anything I done. Luck was on my side, that was all, and I took full advantage.

The doors was closed, but lucky for me, one of them push buttons for the elderly and wheelchair bound was installed at the top of the wooden ramp running up the side of the steps. It took me a few tries to figure out how to stand on my two hindlegs long enough to smack a paw against that button, and lordy, what a sight that musta been.

Finally, though, I done the deed and the doors swung open on a mechanical whir. I slid inside, grateful for the narrowness of my new body, and nearly run smack dab into another witch. Outta instinct more'n anything, I swiped a paw at her, batting her leg through thick denim jeans. She scrambled back and throwed up her hands, and I launched myself straight at her, reveling in the easy power of strong muscles and lithe grace.

I hit her in the chest, right between the magic gathering in her open palms, and down we both went. She rolled to the side and her breath sorta spurted outta her, and I went tumbling legs over back along the slick floor. My front paws yanked back. I glanced around and nearly groaned. My claws was tangled up in the long, loose ends of her wispy blonde hair, ruining the careful curls.

Which begged the question as to what kind of person curled her hair before heading into a fight, but I shelved that'un, too, and got on with it.

She muttered a string of curses, wrapped her hands around her hair, and yanked right as I jerked my claw-tipped paws back. I come away with a wad of blonde hair, shook it free, then before she could regain her senses, pounced on her.

What was the good of being a painter if a body couldn't do a little pouncing?

She landed flat on her back. Her head rebounded into the floor and she winced, then her hands shot up again, glowing blue tinged with black. Casual as could be, I swiped her again, claws out, and knocked her hands aside, scoring deep gouges in her skin. She gasped and paled, her eyes round and fixed on my upright paw.

I should kill her now.

The urge to do just that gathered in my innards, pounding through me with ever beat of my heart. My paw twitched as I considered her, and her fear filled my nostrils with its rancid odor. Kill her now and that was one less unfriendly witch I'd have at my back. I was so used to killing monsters, the hesitation to do it now kindly surprised me.

Kill her now, that was my instinct. Just one swipe of my paw across her exposed throat. The red would flow out of her, spilling across the floor, and it was the red I needed, the red I was supposed to follow.

189

Red magic, not blood.

I reared back, appalled at my own thoughts. This witch weren't no monster. I woulda smelled the evil on her if she was, that was a certainty. She was a human being caught up in strange loyalties and didn't deserve to die for picking the wrong side.

Didn't mean I shouldn't scare her straight.

I placed my paws flat on either side of her head, letting the claws dig into her chest a little as I moved 'em so she'd feel it for a while, and stuck my snout right up against her nose so our eyes met.

Then I growled, real soft and deep in my throat.

Her eyes rolled back in her head and she passed out, my hand to God. I snuffled at her, sniffing along her throat just to make sure she weren't faking it, but nope, she was out cold.

Time to get a move on.

I stepped around her, careful to do no more damage than what I already done, and ignored the tiny drops of her blood dripping off the tips of my claws.

The kids was here, Nora said, but where?

I lifted my snout and sniffed delicately. Scents flooded me, overwhelming my senses. The astringent bite of pine cleaner mingled with freshly cut wood. Half a dozen perfumes ranging from floral to musky hung in the air. Deodorant soap, paper, printer ink, worn leather, ammonia, humidity, fabric softener, starched shirts, moss, and what felt like hundreds of other smells jumbled together in my nostrils, fighting for supremacy.

I bowed my head and batted my snout with a paw, trying to clear the clutter. Somewhere inside me, a new voice emerged, something ancient and wise what felt vaguely like my daddy's daddy.

Take one scent, he whispered. *Forget the rest.*

His voice was like a broom whisking over a hardwood floor, soft and sibilant, soothing, and so hypnotic, I lowered my paw and tried again.

190

Sniff.

A burning fire, crackling in the fireplace. Polyester stuffed pillows encased in handwoven linen.

Sniff.

Nora's perfume, that light, herbal scent she favored.

Sniff.

Sheets of paper, fresh off the printer. Plastic binders. Metal staples.

Sniff.

Red magic.

My head popped up and tilted toward that smell. Brenyn smelled like that, and her brothers, and the woods where the kids went a-missing. It was all over the place, some new, some old. The new was likely left over from them walking across the lobby just now, but the old...

What if I followed them? Would they lead me to them young'uns?

Only one way to find out.

But first, I needed to let the gang know.

I squinched my eyes shut and felt along that thread tying me and Libby together 'til it was firm in my mind. Instead of trying to talk (and lordy, wouldn't that've been something), I shoved the red magic smell at her and hoped like the dickens she understood what I meant.

Then I opened my eyes and sniffed again, searching for the red among the many smells clogging my nose, and away I went, feeling more like a bloodhound than a two-natured beast.

NOISE FROM the fight cut off behind me when the main doors clicked shut. The silence was almost deafening after all the hullabaloo. I cocked my head, listened for a minute. Here and there a shout drifted through, dampened by the thick wooden doors and distance, but inside, all was quiet, still, hollow.

Satisfied that I was alone, or as alone as I could be, I surveyed the lobby again, trying to get my bearings. Hallways branched off the main lobby, mirrored to the right and the left in broad, open spaces wide enough for five folks to walk abreast without their shoulders touching. I went right, following one other trace of the red magic what was faint and dim under the other smells. Instinct, too. It was there, calling to me, some underlying feeling guiding me along.

I couldn't pinpoint *why*, though, and I was sure there was a why.

The floor was cool against my paws, hard, ungiving. There was a gloss to it I never felt with my human feet, never give it a second thought nohow. It was the newness of it all. Maybe when I was a babe newborn, I felt the same way, but if I did, it was lost to time and memory.

I reveled in it now, in the slide of my paws along the shiny surface, in their give against the wood, in the deep scent of lumber underlying a fresh coat of paint. It was all new to me, fresh, like I never seen it before, never experienced it. I wanted to lay down and wallow, squirming along the floor from one end of the hallway to t'other 'til the scent coated ever hair on my body and become a part of me.

The *why* tugged at me, pulling me along, and I let the notion of wallowing slip away.

Maybe another day.

The red magic dipped into this room or that down the hallway. I stuck my head into the open doorways, snooping on the contents, and pawed open closed, lever-handled doors. Most of the rooms was offices arranged in neat little arrays of wooden desks and book-lined walls and ancient, squishy rugs thrown across the floors.

Me, I was content with my ocean blue shag carpeting. It mighta been older'n dirt and it mighta been touched by the magic of a demigod, but it was one hundred percent mine.

I come to the end of the hallway without discovering much. The red magic drifted in and outta some of the offices, but them was newer smells. The older thread ended at a metal door with a sturdy doorknob holding it in place.

Well, dang. I needed human hands for doorknobs, not paws. The ring made me a painter, but how could I take it off when I didn't even have fingers right now?

Hunh. Guess I shoulda thought of that before I put the dadgum thing on.

I snuffled a half laugh through my snout, and twisted around, heading back toward the lobby and human help.

A woman was standing halfway down the hall, blocking my route back, her long black hair pulled into a ponytail high on the back of her head. She was all in black, like the rest of them witches what'd attacked us, and her hands was held loose at her sides, bracketing an athletic body.

Thing was, I hadn't heard her walking behind me, hadn't sensed her, couldn't smell her. She'd popped up without me even knowing. Where in tarnation did she come from?

Or was she even really there?

Only one way to find out. I snarled at her good, then bunched my hindlegs up and leapt forward into a run.

To her credit, she held her ground, but her eyes got about as round as saucers, which answered one question. Yup, she was real, or real enough to ken what threat a painter was, even a new'un like me.

I didn't slow down. The way I figured it, if I give her any room to think on it, she'd have them hands up shooting sparks of magic at me. That was the last thing I wanted, so I went at her full speed, gangly legs and all, and didn't stop even when I got close. No, sirree, I planned on barreling her over, and I woulda, too.

If she'd really been there.

Soon as my nose touched her, she dissipated into wispy black smoke and disappeared. I skidded to a stop on t'other side of where she been, sliding across the polished floor 'til my butt hit a wall, then my body, and finally my noggin.

Pain blossomed across my temple and I shook my head.

Ouch. That'd hurt a mite more'n I figured it would, but I was more concerned with what'd happened to that woman than I was with what'd happened to my head. Was that a spell of some sort she'd used to, I dunno, project into the hallway, or did she really just up and disappear on me?

Right about then, something swooshed and the noise from the fight suddenly got loud again. Footsteps rang out, echoing through the lobby into the hallway, and a man said, "I'll go right."

I sighed, which ain't as easy when you're a painter as when you're a human, believe you me.

A woman said, "I'm on the l—oh, shit!"

I snickered and untangled myself from the wall as a quick series of pops sounded from the lobby. Riley hollered, "Sunny!" Then the man I encountered when the fighting first broke out rounded the corner, hell bent for leather. His hand lifted into the air and an eerie green light gathered around it.

Uh oh.

I struggled to my feet and squared off against him, my head down as a low growl gathered in my throat.

21

The first burst of green light shot out before I could even brace for it. It hit me dead on, right in the chest, and tumbled me over backwards. My whole body went numb, and that scared me more'n pain woulda. Pain I could handle. Numb left me weak and useless.

I couldn't feel the floor beneath me.

The man walked over, his beautiful mouth twisted into a wry smile. He nudged me with a booted toe, then squatted beside me and held his hand out over my snout, about two inches from my nose. "Well, that was a little too easy. You in there? I know you can hear me."

I shifted my head back, though I couldn't feel it slide along the floor. Let me tell you, that was the weirdest sensation, moving my head without being able to feel it.

The man laughed and his hand disappeared behind my eyes, toward my nape. "You're not going anywhere, pretty little kitty. I know who you are. Watched you transform.

Amazing magic, that. Maybe I'll steal it from you before I skin you alive. Your pelt would make a nice addition to my collection."

Fear turned my heart to ice, even as it leapt into a full-blown gallop in my chest.

Odd that I could feel it when I couldn't even feel my own paws.

The smile dropped off his face and his expression tightened. He put his head real close to mine and whispered, "Or maybe I'll steal your magic and keep you as my human pet. Would you like to be chained to my bed, kitty?"

Behind him somewhere, the fight raged on, drowning out whatever he said next, but I didn't need to hear the words to get the gist. Men had talked like that to me before, men what'd gone on to limp for a good spell after I got through with 'em.

But I'd had the benefit of full movement then, not this wasting numbness tingling through my body.

He leaned back, smiling that thin, cruel grin at me, and his eyes was like ice in his narrow face. "One more thing, pet. *Cloch.*"

My body stiffened, like rigor mortis set into my limbs. Worse, 'cause now the numbness was gone and I could feel his hand ruffling through my fur, petting me. It woulda give me a good case of the willies if I weren't as stone cold stiff as a statue, and if I hadn't realized something horrible right then.

My heart'd stopped beating. My lungs didn't seem to be working neither, and if they wasn't, then my blood stopped circulating and no telling what else weren't working right.

Panic rippled through me as suffocation pressed down on me hard. I was gonna die there in that hallway, and I was gonna feel ever bit of death's icy scythe when the grim reaper come to take my soul.

I was never gonna see Riley again, never gonna kiss him, never tell him I loved him. And Fame and Missy and them, what was they gonna think when they found my body laying here, already dead and gone?

My sight dimmed and withered, and a great hand pressed harder on my lungs. I wanted to open my mouth and gasp in air, wanted to claw and scream and fight for the life this man'd denied me. Most of all, I wanted to rip my way through the man's body, hold him down and tear flesh from bone one sharp-toothed bite at a time.

All I could do was lay there and wait for my body to shut down one organ at a time, and rage against the hand this man had dealt me.

How dare he do this to me? What right did he have to kill me in such a horrible manner?

The man put his hands on my lower jaw and pried it open, then he breathed into my mouth. Air filled my lungs and they expanded against an unmoving chest, pressing so hard, it felt like something burst and bruised inside me. Couldn't complain, though, could I? I was breathing again, my heart was beating. I was still stiff as granite, but I wouldn't die of it now.

His hand slid over my eyes, closing 'em, then a small breeze whirled around me and he was gone. Leastwise, I couldn't feel him no more, so I figured he rejoined the battle. It was odd just laying there, hearing the fighting, hearing Riley and Fame and all the rest but not being able to do nothing about it.

Well, I did something, all right. I committed that man's features to memory. One of the brothers, I figured, or maybe not, but either way, it didn't matter. Soon as I was freed from whatever spell he cast on me, I was gonna hunt his sorry hide down and skin it good, and then we'd see whose pelt ended up gracing whose floor.

I WAS AWARE of the fighting in the way of somebody hid behind a curtain while the main show played out across the stage. It was there, just beyond my senses, but the main action was beyond me.

Something else tickled my awareness, too, somewhere out of reach of my own struggle to breathe without bursting a lung. A soft whisper, a gentle nudge, the merest suggestion of movement in my mind.

Gradually, the world around me dimmed, drowned out by that deeper part of me, and it all pointed to one thing I done forgot. I was still wearing Missy's ring.

Now, what that had to do with anything, I hadn't a clue, but that little tidbit kept pushing itself to the forefront of my mind. Her ring was still on my finger, though it was a part of my painter paw now same as the glossy black fur covering my skin. It was a magic ring, the very same one what'd pushed me over the threshold from human to painter. What kind of power it possessed, Missy hadn't rightly explained. Leastwise, I never pinned it down beyond that its benefits was mostly individual. Something was there, thought, something I was missing.

It was a magic ring.

Magic ring.

Magic.

And it was supposed to guard against enchantments.

Which begged the question as to why I was sprawled out on the dadgum floor under the influence of a powerful spell, but go figure. A body works with what the Good Lord gives her.

I concentrated hard on the band of gold circling my finger, now absorbed into my painter nature. In my mind's eye, I pictured it. My hand, the human one, wearing that ring. Gold against brown flesh, the red wink of the square cut ruby flashing in the sunlight. Then the painter I was now, and back again to my human self.

Which give me an idea. What if I could be human again, if the ring could make me human again? Would that confound the spell that man laid on me, the one what'd turned me to stone?

The way I figured it, it was worth a shot. Shoot, anything was better'n laying here waiting on the ring to work its magic when it was good and ready to.

Or worse, waiting on that scoundrel to come back and claim what little magic I got.

I pulled up my human self again in my mind's eye, nekkid me with my flat butt and barely there breasts and straight as a stick brown-black hair, and I didn't stop with the physical. Why, no, I couldn't stop there, seeing as how that was only a part of me, so I kept going to them things most folk never seen. The coon crazy inherited from my mama, the kind heart give by my daddy. The love I shared with Henry, and now Riley, and the shaping done by Fame and Trey and Gentry, and even Missy, the woman what'd been as much a mama to me as the woman what'd birthed me.

And the newer stuff, too. The blood on my hands from killing so many monsters, my friendship with BobbiJean and Jazz and their baby yet to be, and with David, him what kept sneaking kisses in when Riley weren't looking. Young Billy Kildare and them infernal dogs of his, and Aunt Sadie and her kin. What my grandma Walkingstick done to me and mine, and what Johnny done to make it right. Libby and her brood, lost family found, and on and on 'til a thousand threads shot through me.

Them threads swelled to life inside me, fleshing out my shape, and a tingling started in my paw, right where that ring resided, as much a part of me as anything else I thought on. And as I looked at them threads, examining the flow and pattern of 'em weaving through my life, I realized how wrong I always been about my place on the earthly plane.

I weren't alone. I never had been.

A teary happiness burst through me, carrying that tingling along with it, and sweet, dark pain ripped me apart, waking up that which was turned to stone. Muscle flexed over bone, fur absorbed into flesh made anew, and magic jittered in me, turning me inside out. Not the magic of the ring, but the magic what'd always been a part of me, just never strong enough to exert itself over the pragmatic Carson side of me.

I laughed in spite of myself, and to my utter relief and sorrow both, it sounded human to my ears. My eyelids popped open and I uncurled my human self and looked around. First thing I seen was that ring glittering on my finger, then my nekkid arm, and it didn't take much brain power for me to figure out it weren't the only nekkid part of me.

No time for dwelling on the lack of clothes. The battle still raged in flashes of light and the occasional grunted curse. I needed to find them young'uns lickety split while the rest of them fighting was occupied elsewhere.

22

I kept Missy's ring on my finger. The chain done broke and even if I could fix it, I weren't in no mood to hunt for it. That'd be like searching for a needle in a haystack while the Army and Navy played war games around the hayfield.

So the ring was my only adornment as I pushed myself into a wobbly stand and headed for the door where the older red magic trail disappeared. My bare feet was silent on the floor, or silent enough under the fighting coming from the lobby. By the sounds of it, I reckoned I was under the influence of that statue spell for less time than it felt like.

The doorknob turned easy enough in my human hands, though it felt a mite weird not having paws, and opened on a brightly lit flight of stairs. One set went up, t'other down, and it was down I headed now, bouncing along the stairs as fast as I dared whilst the door swung shut and once again the hullabaloo was silenced.

In fact, it was so quiet down here, it was spooky. I rubbed chills off my arms and exited in the lowest floor, a sub basement two floors below ground level. The door was marked by a sign reading *Archives*, and that was the perfect spot for it, assuming somebody'd figured out a way to keep it from flooding.

Hey, I weren't in charge of the rain, but we sure did get enough of it.

I entered a shallow foyer of sorts opening into a maze of dim, narrow hallways and hooked my hands on my hips. Well, for crying out loud. How was a body supposed to find anything in that mess?

I shivered right about then and shrugged. Nothing for it. I was gonna have to brave the cooler air nekkid as the day I was born, but which way to go first?

I sniffed the air, searching for the red magic over the scent of dank earth. Surprisingly enough, my sniffer worked almost as good as it had when I was a painter, and slowly, I sorted out one smell from another. Glass jars and pottery full of dried herbs. Paper and ink and an odd scent like leather, but not any kind of leather I ever smelled before. Wax and dead fires, ash and coals. Pine, freshly cut, and metal. Iron, to be exact.

There, that inner voice said, and my feet automatically followed, veering me off into a passage two hallways from the foyer's right-hand wall. Another scent accompanied the iron, and as I wandered down the twisting passage, passing beneath antique electric sconces placed just far enough apart for darkness to inhabit the spaces between lights, I began to place the smell.

Or smells, to be exact. Sweat and urine and denim and rubber, and underlying it all, the salt-tinged scent of tears.

Them young'uns.

My heart leapt forward, aiming toward them smells, and my feet followed, quick as a rabbit outrunning the fox. The red magic trail growed stronger, oddly enough, and so did the smell of them young'uns. Not the sounds, though. It was still quiet as a tomb, and that scared me.

What if I was too late?

I rounded a bend going full-bore right into a hollow the size of a bear's den, and nearly tumbled elbow over arse in an effort to stop. Beyond, the hollow widened into a shadow-filled, cavernous room, the front part of which looked like it was carved from the natural bedrock. Iron bars blocked the passage between the two around a door made of the same, but that weren't what stopped me. No, that'd be the woman standing between me and the bars, smiling coldly at me from not ten feet away.

Brenyn.

How in tarnation did she get down here ahead of me?

I shook that question away and squared off to her. "You best move outta the way now, Brenyn. I aim to get them young'uns and take 'em home."

Her smile widened into an evil grin. "And I aim to sacrifice them under the dark of the moon. Shall we see which of us prevails?"

Up her hands come as she shot a ball of magic at me, but I done wised up to that little trick and I was getting tired of it to boot. Unfortunately, my best weapon was laying two floors above us in the parking lot, where I shed my clothes, and I had no idea how to transform back into a painter, if that was even a good idea in this particular situation.

Nothing for it, then. I was gonna have to use the weapons I was born with.

I ducked the first spray of Brenyn's magic, a ghostly smoke colored blob what give me the heebies as it sailed over my head, and inched forward even as I surveyed the space for anything what could help me. Shoot, I'd even take an old book at this point. Least I could throw it at her and maybe distract her some.

The walls was nigh on bare. No shelves here, no drapes, no nothing outside of a coupla low crates along one wall and a decrepit wooden bench set against t'other. I ducked an electric blue orb what sorta floated at me, sidestepped a red spray, and each time I stepped a little closer to her, 'til by the time she tried that same green thing on me that man'd done, I was right on top of her.

I knocked her arm outta the way with one hand and punched her solid in the nose with my other'n.

Which served her right, the hussy. That's what she got for flinging her shiny, sparkly magic at me.

She flinched back and her hands come to her nose, not even remotely stopping the blood gushing down her mouth.

I grinned and jabbed her again, this time in the jaw, and man, oh man, was it satisfying to watch her head pop around.

She flailed her hands without looking and slapped a blood-covered palm against my upper arm. Pain seared through me as my flesh bubbled and burned under her touch. I yelped and wrenched away from her, then shoved her hard into the iron bars.

She slid straight down onto the floor and muttered, "Bitch."

"Right back atcha," I said, not muttering one bit.

She peered at me through bleary eyes. "Give up now. You're no match for me."

"Oh, yeah? I guess that's why you're sitting there in the dirt while I'm standing here figuring out which part of you I'm gonna dismantle first."

"Vicious dog."

"That's vicious cat to you, Miss Priss," I said, and kicked her legs to the side, making dadgum sure her butt stayed planted. "Still think you're gonna win this'un?"

"I always win," she said. "That's how I've survived all these centuries."

Her fingers wiggled at me, and danged if my throat didn't seize up, cutting off my air.

What was it with these witches and suffocating a body?

Now, I coulda clawed at my throat or whatnot, but the

way I figured it, if I knocked her out cold, the magic would work itself out. That or the ring'd show me how to shed the spell.

So being the coon crazy woman I was, I reared back and clocked her good, ignoring the pain of lungs straining for air and the bruises on my knuckles. I'd die before I let her crawl outta here in one piece.

Thing was, I weren't ready to die. It was good to know that while my body used up the oxygen stored in my lungs and blood, and the reaper waited in the wings, patient as death.

The reaper being patient as death. That tickled my funny bone.

"*Desino*," a voice called behind me, and the breath rushed into my lungs, filling a void so deep, I nearly choked on it. My feet tangled together reflexively and I tottered outta the way, then Missy popped into view, her hands held chest high, her violet eyes glowing as her sable hair floated around her pale, pale face.

"MOVE, SUNNY," Missy said.

"I'm a-going as fast—"

Brenyn's bloody hands whipped out, throwing a wide burst of sickly yellow light at us. The leading edge hit me and lifted me into the air, then dumped me against the left wall. I crashed into the crates butt first, cursing ever splinter what'd buried itself in my hide the whole time.

Missy deflected the magic and somehow transformed it into another spell and shot it back again. It caught Brenyn by the throat and her mouth gaped wide, like all the oxygen was sucked outta her lungs.

Karma is a bitch.

I scrambled upright, trying my darnedest to ignore the bruises blooming across my bare hide. "Missy, the bars!"

Brenyn gasped in a breath then, and on the exhale,

wheezed out, "*Flagello.*"

Thin red lines crisscrossed Missy's face and she stumbled back, one hand held out behind a hastily conjured, barely there shield. I jumped on the opportunity to get a little of my own back against Brenyn and happily slapped her forehead hard, shooting the back of her head into the iron bar right behind her. Her nails clawed at my arm, doing more damage than was warranted by fingernails, and I figured she put some magic into her scrapes, or maybe the blood clotting on her hands held some kinda witchy poison.

What did I know? I still hadn't done enough research on witches to ken their magic, and was getting enough first-hand experience to make up for it.

Though I woulda dearly loved to know what them foreign sounding words meant outside what I could see with my own two eyes.

I backhanded Brenyn, and without waiting for her to recover from that head whip, reached up and yanked on the padlock holding the door shut. It stayed firmly shut, and I nearly cursed aloud.

Dang it all. A little luck woulda gone a long way right then.

Brenyn reached for me again, but a shot of pure azure sliced into her, literally scoring a hole through her shoulder. She screamed and her hands dropped away, just as another beam cut into her, two inches closer to her black heart and not six inches away from my thigh, so close the heat of it seared my skin.

"Missy," I hollered. "Watch where you're aiming that!"

"Get out of the way," she said, just as another blue beam shot toward me. I fell down and away from Brenyn, something sizzled, and the smell of super hot metal filled the small space.

I looked up. The lower half of the padlock was gone. The upper half, the curved part holding the door shut, was cooling from red hot to steaming black.

Whoo-wee! If I'da knowed Missy could do that, I woulda kept my nose a whole heckuva lot cleaner.

Brenyn raised both her hands and kinda pushed her palms toward Missy. Red tendrils shot out and wound their way around her just as Missy shoved a blood orange mass of magic toward Brenyn. Missy's arms fell to her side and her face drained of color, then she slowly slid into a limp heap in the doorway as Brenyn gasped and arched her back and fell to her side on the floor.

23

"**M**issy!" I screamed as I scrambled across the room and dropped to her side. My fingers trembled along her neck, found a threadbare pulse, and I half-sobbed, half-laughed my relief.

Footsteps pounded along the hallways, drawing near, but the situation was clear to me, so crystal clear. Missy was dying. I could feel her life force fading under my fingertips, feel it ebbing away into the dank air.

Memories flooded me, filling my mind, of the day Missy showed up at Fame's, claiming to be a lost hiker when we all knowed she weren't nothing of the kind, just by looking on her voluptuous figure.

Of Missy holding Henry close, cooing out a lullaby to him.

Of Missy holding me when I come back from hunting down that pooka, soaked in blood not my own and so hollow, weren't nothing holding me together but her and Fame and the boys.

Of love shining outta Missy's eyes ever time she looked on my uncle, of the way she brung Gentry outta his shell and fed Trey up. Of her in her hand me downs, trodding barefoot along the path, resting beside Henry's little angel. Of her a thousand times, holding my family together when time and hardship shoulda rent us apart.

Where would we've been without Missy all them long, lonely years?

The ring cooled against my hand, and it was only then that I remembered it. I stared down at it, my eyes so blurred with tears, I could scarce make out the breadth of it. She give me this ring, Missy did, back when that hussy Belinda Arrowood stole it off her neck, right in front of God and ever body. Missy give it to me and told me it was mine.

And that ring'd give me something special. It'd made me whole again, showed me how to be a painter when I never thought on being one. Down deep, I knowed that ring was the only way I'd be a painter again, the only way I'd ever run with my Cherokee kin on four legs, ever share that communion with 'em.

'Twas the only way I'd ever be like my daddy, and his daddy before him, and so on back through time to when that distant ancestor first sat down with the painters and took their magic into her soul, making it an eternal part of herself.

But if I was right, that very ring'd save Missy from the magic slung at her by an ancient dark witch.

I could keep the ring and be what I shoulda been all along, or I could use the ring's power and heal Missy, sacrificing any chance of being whole again, of being something other than a half-breed, white trash, no account woman.

It weren't even a choice in my mind.

I slipped the ring off my own finger and wrapped Missy's palm around it, then I used ever bit of what little magic was mine and willed the ring to do what it could for her. It flared hot and bright between us, nigh on scorching my skin and hers both. I held on for dear life, praying like I hadn't prayed since Henry died.

Please, God, let this work. Please let this be Your will.

And whether God was listening or not, that ring sure was. It glowed so bright, I had to close my eyes against it, then the glow went out and Missy's eyes popped open on a gasp.

I looked up and saw Fame and Riley and the sheriff crowded into the doorway behind Nora, who was holding one arm against her chest, and painter Libby. My gaze met Fame's, and in that small space of time, I read the thank you in his wild blue eyes.

I nodded and let my hands fall away from Missy. She was gonna be ok now, but there was still work to do here, starting with finishing off Brenyn and seeing what was behind them iron bars.

I NEEDN'T'VE worried about Brenyn. By the time Fame carted Missy off, held tight to his chest, and Nora limped into the room to check on Brenyn, life had fled, leaving the dark witch's body an empty, rapidly decaying shell. I reckoned time finally caught up to her, the way it did to ever thing along and along. I let that thought wither before it planted itself in my noggin. Last thing I needed was thoughts of death and dying added to the burden I carried.

Riley shrugged off his flannel shirt and draped it over my shoulders, then him and his daddy dragged Brenyn outta the way. Soon as she was clear, I flicked the remains of the padlock off the iron bars and took ahold of the door.

It swung open soundlessly, and me and Nora stepped through, leaving Libby to change back into human form. Nora flicked her fingers out as she limped along beside me, and little balls of light shot through the air, hanging above and in front of us, shedding enough light to make the cavern look like the sun rose up inside it.

I slid my arms into the sleeves of Riley's shirt, savoring the body heat clinging to it from where he'd worn it, and glanced around. Wooden and plastic boxes lined the far wall, which weren't near as far back as I first thought, and right in front of that, laying in small cages meant for dogs and the like, was the missing young'uns.

I grunted. Somehow, I thought it'd be harder than this, once we got through the iron bars, but maybe Brenyn figured them and the cages was enough.

Still, my blood boiled on seeing them young'uns locked up like animals. I hurried to 'em, but Nora was one step ahead of me. Already, the fingers of her good hand flicked out, snapping locks in two with an invisible force guided by her magic. I come along behind her and opened the cages, then coaxed sleeping young'uns out and passed 'em back to Libby and t'others what'd drifted in behind her to help with the rescue.

I recognized each one from their pictures, of course, Mikey and Isabella and all the rest, but a couple of 'em tugged at me good. Wyatt stirred and woke as I got to his cage. Soon as I opened the door, he crawled out on his own and flung his arms around me, whispering in his little boy's voice how even though he was scared, he'd knowed we was coming for him.

"I told 'em to be brave," he said, then Libby snatched him outta my arms and squeezed him to her nekkid chest so hard, he huffed out a plaintive, "Mama, let go!"

"Not ever again," she replied, and I nearly cried right then and there, the memory of my own boy's loss hit me so hard.

One by one, we freed them young'uns, and one by one, they passed by me 'til I got to the very end and the little girl sleeping so peaceful and calm in the last cage. That *other* tugged at me again, and of a sudden, it hit me what it'd been: A magic borne of shared kinship and the love we both held for a little boy we lost too soon.

This, as much as the red magic, was what'd led me down

here, that tenuous bond I shared with my boy's half-sister. In her own way, she saved herself, and that bore some thinking on when I possessed the brain power to start thinking again.

I reached into the cage and placed my hand on her ankle. "Sophie, honey. Time to go."

She woke and looked up at me, and a slow grin spread across her pretty face. "Henry said you was coming for me."

I startled at that and my eyes got real big. "You mean Wyatt, honey?"

She shook her head and crawled out to me, then her arms went around my neck and we held onto each other for a good long while, me and the sister my boy'd never knowed.

I CARRIED little Sophie out past a line of my Cherokee kin, murmuring thanks but no thanks when a few offered to hold Sophie for me. I just needed a little time with her, a little more time sharing the love Henry left us both with, even if she'd never felt it. Tears streamed down my face, blurring my vision so much, I nearly stumbled, but a hand was firm at my elbow ever time, leading me down the hallway, up the stairs, and past a slew of zip tied witches sprawled all over the lodge's main floor.

Red and blue lights flashed from the tops of squad cars, lighting up the moonless night. Later, Riley told me his daddy'd called the fight and us finding the missing kids in to the local police. Right then, I didn't care. I was just grateful for the EMTs looking us and the kids over, for the spouses and friends of the First Responders bringing out hot chocolate and hotter coffee for us, and most of all for the blankets somebody fetched and wrapped around us all.

By golly, it was chilly out, especially for them of us what was still nekkid, or mostly so.

I never learnt what Sheriff Treadwell said to the White County sheriff to explain away what'd happened, and I never cared. An EMT tried to part me and Sophie, but she hollered so much, he asked me to stand beside her, holding her hand while he checked her over. Soon as she was done, I sat down, and she crawled into my lap while the EMT bandaged my arm where Brenyn burned it.

For once, I was none the worse for wear, likely 'cause ever body kept telling me to duck and otherwise run interference for me, but the guilt of the injuries my family and friends sustained during the fight ate away at me. We didn't lose nobody, though, and that's what I tried to focus on.

In war, there's a lot to be said for nobody dying but the bad guy. Or gal, in this case.

Riley was beside me the whole time. They left the remnants of Brenyn's body in the hallway for the police to find, though Nora whispered an aside to me that it wasn't enough. She needed to be burned. Otherwise, her brothers might try to resurrect her through some dark ritual, and after what we went through, no way in hell was we letting that happen.

Especially since the brothers had up and disappeared on us.

Trey told us later they just vanished right outta their zip ties, which begged the question as to how we got them dadgum plastic things on 'em in the first place. But I weren't thinking too hard on it, aside from tucking away my vow of revenge on the one brother.

Strange that I never smelled the red magic on him while he was working his spells on me, though of a certainty, he was steeped in the stuff.

We all piled into vehicles any which way we could and headed out to the local hospital and the sheriff's office, which ever one we was individually needed at. I endured a coupla officers taking my statement, watched bemused as the same officers tried to get statements from a bunch of Snowbird Cherokee what suddenly couldn't speak a word of English.

Woulda laughed if I'da had the energy for it.

Mostly I sat beside Sophie in the conference room the

sheriff begged from a local bank and waited on her parents to come get her while night fell asleep and the day woke, in a magic so old and timeless, we humans scarce thought on it as magic at all.

24

The police started calling parents soon as they matched each young'un to a missing kid report. Libby and her family left long before that, though she took the time to hunt me down and say goodbye before then. We'd talk again. She didn't need to say it for me to understand. Right now, her place was at home with her family. The rest could come later.

Sophie fell asleep long before her parents got there, so she missed her daddy bursting into the conference room looking like he was dragged through a knothole backwards. Her mama rushed through right behind him and made a beeline for Sophie, and Terry tagged along wide-eyed and dazed, his eyes brimming with tears.

Ellie swept Sophie up and held her tight, nigh on bawling as Sophie woke and realized who held her.

Terry stumbled up to me and held out his hand. "Sunny, I..."

I stood up, grasped his hands between mine, and looked

him straight in the face. "You don't gotta say nothing, Terry."

"I do. Sunny. I..." He swiped his free hand over his face, smudging tears over the bags under his eyes, and when he looked at me again, something akin to regret shone from him. "I shouldn'ta left you like I done, shouldn'ta left my boy without his daddy. You don't know how much I wanted to beg you to let me be a part of his life, any part, you know? I woulda taken anything if I thought you'd let me have it."

I couldn't say nothing to that. Maybe I was still bitter over the way Terry done me and Henry, or maybe I just didn't have the words right then. I conjured some up anyhow, the first words I could lay my mind to. "He was a good young'un, Terry. Any man woulda been proud to call him son."

"I was, Sunny," Terry said, and that was good enough to ease some of the hurt still lingering in my heart.

I'd never have my Henry back. I'd never know that kinda love again, but I still had a part of him here on Earth in little Sophie and her baby brother. That much I could hold onto, and it healed a wounded part of me what'd been buried so deep, I hadn't even knowed it was there.

Sophie lunged outta her mama's arms right then, straight at me, and I give her one last good hug before she moved on to her daddy. "You're coming to my birthday party, ain'tcha?" she said. Ellie laughed and said as how I'd better be there, and Terry just shook his head and grinned at me, and I said yes as Riley sidled up to me and draped a possessive arm around my shoulders.

Bless him, he'd been through as much as I had, though the brunt of it didn't sink into my head the first time he told me, right there in the conference room once Terry took his young family home.

The bandages wrapped around his wrists alarmed me about as much as the scrapes on his face, but he squeezed me close and kissed my forehead and told me he'd explain again later.

Somebody found my clothes and returned 'em to me. They was so dirty from laying in the parking lot, I just tossed 'em in the back of Riley's SUV and shimmied into the spare pair I brung down as Riley drove me to the hospital.

We seen Nora first. She was being kept overnight in a semiprivate room she just been admitted to when we snuck in past security and a bevy of overprotective night nurses.

I weren't gonna wait for nobody's permission after what we been through. And I had my own wounds to nurse, the faint ache in my lungs and throat from being magically suffocated, the scrapes and bruises from being tossed into them crates, and half a dozen other aches and injuries I was sure to notice in a day or two.

When me and Riley slipped into her room, Nora was resting in her bed, her face turned toward the window across the room's other hospital bed, tidily made and empty. Her blonde hair was matted and dirt streaked, and bruises splotched across her face and neck above the hospital gown she wore. A temporary cast was strapped around her left forearm. There was more. There had to be, after the night we had.

I took the chair beside her bed and Riley propped his back against the door, ensuring at least a good notice before we was interrupted.

"How you feeling?" I said, gentle as I could.

She wiped the tears pooling under her eyes, though her gaze stayed on the morning light peeping through the blinds. "As well as I can, considering that I just betrayed my entire coven."

I put my hand on her knee through the thin hospital sheet and shook it just enough to catch her attention. "Hey, now. You saved thirteen young'uns from a terrible fate tonight. That's gotta count for something."

"Not to them. You don't know..." Her eyelids slid shut and she shook her head wearily. "They'll cast me out of the coven."

217

"Good riddance to that bunch of rattlesnakes," I said, kindly firm. "You're better off on your own."

"You don't understand. A witch without a coven is—" She squinched her face up into a grimace, struggling, I thought, to find a way to explain it to me. "We're defenseless on our own, vulnerable. That's why we band together, for protection from those who seek to destroy us."

"But you ain't on your own, Nora," I said, still aiming for gentle. "I ain't no witch, but you got me just the same."

She looked at me for a long moment, then her lips twitched into a smile and she laughed. "Oh, Sunny. If anyone had told me that someday I'd have a half-two-natured at my back, I would've smacked them into the next decade."

Riley snickered behind me, but I just grinned and said, "Welcome to the next decade, Nora Vargas," and laughed so hard, I hurt my bruised ribs all over again.

MISSY WAS waiting for us by the time we snuck past the changing of the guards and got to her room. She was sitting up in bed holding Fame's hand, looking bright eyed and bushy tailed in spite of what Brenyn pulled on her.

Riley followed me into her room and let the door swing shut behind him. My gaze flicked between her and Fame and back again. "You ok?"

"Never better." She patted the bed beside her thigh. "Come sit with me, darling."

"I'll take a chair, thanks." And I did, sliding one across the room and positioning it opposite Fame, though I did place a hand careful like on her forearm, above the IV needle stuck in the back of her hand. "Them nurses treating you good?"

Her expression softened into a smile. "Why, Sunny. You were truly worried, weren't you?"

I scowled at her, somewhat taken aback. "'Course I was. Brenyn nearly done you in."

Fame reached across Missy's lap and laid his hand on mine. "You saved her."

"Well, what in tarnation was I supposed to do?"

Riley's hands fell on my shoulder and smoothed over them, like he was trying to soothe me before my temper got too riled. "How about some breakfast? I'm starving."

Fame squeezed my hand, then stood and nodded. "I can come with you. Need to stretch my legs anyhow, now that Sunny's here to watch over Missy for me."

"Watch over her," I muttered, but Missy just smiled her angelic smile and accepted Fame's peck on her cheek as her due.

Soon as him and Riley was outta the room, I leaned forward and said, "How's the baby?"

Missy patted her tummy through the sheet draped over her. "Safe and sound. An OB-GYN has already come in and given me an ultrasound."

"You got one of them pictures?"

"Fame has it, darling, but as soon as he's back, I'll make him show it to you."

I nodded once, then glanced at the blinds covering the dawning sunshine and the clouds threatening in the distance.

"The ring's power is spent," she said after a minute.

"I figured." Least, that's what it'd felt like after, when Missy gasped her way back from death's sharp edge. "You ok with that?"

"I'm ready to be normal, to have a family. I want to leave the past behind and grow old with someone I love." She placed her free hand over mine and smiled that gentle smile at me. Missy possessed a dozen different smiles and seemed to come up with a new one ever time the occasion called for it. "The question is, are you ok with it?"

I gaped at her, so surprised my tongue froze in my mouth for a second. Took me a minute to unstick it, but when I did, I said, "Why wouldn't I be?"

"Because I know what the ring did for you. I know what

you gave up."

My mouth snapped shut and I just stared at her. "What was it exactly I give up?"

"You know, darling," she said, and danged if her voice didn't gentle down to that of mama to child. "The chance to use the magic you were born with, to be part of something meaningful and good."

"But I am!" I shook my head, bemused. "I'm already part of something meaningful and good, have been since Fame took me in. I got two brothers in Trey and Gentry, and I got you and Fame, and soon, that little'un will be along and no telling what else the years'll bring."

"But you will never be able to transform into a panther again."

Now, that I did regret a mite, but not so much I'd trade it for her life, or any other, for that matter. I searched for a way to tell her she meant more to me'n that ol' painter anyhow, but the words fell short in my mind and my heart couldn't bridge the distance. "I weren't able to transform before, so it ain't like I was used to it or nothing."

Tears welled up in Missy's eyes and her hand tightened on mine. "Oh, Sunny. You have such a good heart."

Danged if a blush didn't heat my cheeks. "I just did what had to be done, is all. You woulda done the same for me."

"Yes, I would've," she said, kindly firm. "I was drawn to you, you know. To the power budding within you."

I cocked my head to the side, purely puzzled by that. "My painter power?"

"No, darling, the power of you. Your goodness, your strength, your love." She sighed and sank back into the pillow propping her upright, and thin lines bracketed her lovely mouth. "Old Mother was, too, and we weren't the only ones. Be careful, darling. More than good follows where power strays."

"You dipping into Old Mother's seeing herbs?"

She laughed, then closed her eyes. "Just a little nap now.

I'm so tired. It's been so long since I rested."

"You go on to sleep now, Missy. I'll watch over you good, you hear?"

But her breathing done relaxed into sleep and she never heard the lullaby I sung her while I looked after her, the way she looked after me since the day her pretty feet brung her home to roost.

RILEY 'BOUT dragged me outta the hospital after we got a good breakfast in us and I made dadgum sure Missy weren't lying about being ok. Bless him, he picked Nora up some breakfast, too, and took it to her, but I didn't learn about that 'til later.

They was lots of things I didn't learn 'til later, as a matter of fact, like what happened with his daddy and Trey and the Cherokee what helped us and the rest of them young'uns we found.

Not to mention the nature camp and the witches and all that.

'Course, I didn't pry too hard. Truth was, I didn't give a good golly fig about them witches by the time he talked me into leaving the hospital so me and him could get some rest.

Good thing he was the persuasive sort, as I was sound asleep before he even drove outta the hospital parking lot. And I didn't wake 'til the Range Rover's tires started bumping up my driveway neither.

"Damn it, Sunny," he said. "You really need to get this road graded."

"I done did," I murmured, still half asleep.

He shot me a skeptical look, then we finally made it to the parking area and into the trailer. I bumped up the heat while he locked up behind us, and we stripped each other down in the bathroom, washed each other up so quick, the water was still steaming hot when we stepped out. Five minutes later, we was dried off and got our teeth brushed, and we fell into bed together, curling around each other like we spent ever night together.

Hours later, and I really couldn't say how long, I woke up to his fingers gently prodding the wound Brenyn burned into me.

I cuddled deeper into Riley, though I stayed right where I was, facing away from him with my eyes shut tight. "It ain't that bad. Splinters in my butt's gotta be worse, anyhow."

A tense silence followed 'stead of the laughter I was aiming for. Finally, Riley pressed a tender kiss to my bare shoulder above the quilt covering us both and said, "No more, Sunny. I can't stand seeing you like this again."

That woke me up good. I half turned against him and looked him square in the face where he was propped up behind me. "You can't stand seeing me like what?"

His fingers plucked at the edge of the bandage the EMT used to patch me up. "Like this. Don't make me go through that again."

I reached for anger or outrage or anything in me what'd take offense at him telling me what to do, and come up completely blank. Maybe I was still too plumb wore out to muster any up, or maybe I was beginning to see where he was coming from. I hadn't rightly liked putting him in harm's way. Sure hadn't liked him volunteering for it neither.

I rolled back over and shut my eyes. "I'll think on it."

He huffed out a laugh against my skin. "That's more than I thought I'd get from you."

"Probably more'n you deserve."

He laughed outright that time. "God, Sunny. What am I gonna do with you?"

I wiggled my butt against his hips, right where a certain part of him was waking up. "You already know the answer to that question."

"Hmm." Another kiss, more soft rubbing along my arm. "Move in with me."

My eyes popped open again. At this rate, they was

beginning to feel a mite like a jack-in-the-box, what with all the stuff Riley was throwing at me. "Where'd that come from?"

"I've been thinking about it for a while, weeks really. I know it's too soon, but it's what I want. I thought, you know." He was silent for a minute, then he said, real soft, "I thought you might want it, too."

I didn't know what I wanted and that's the pure plumb truth, but I weren't mean enough to say it to him, not like that. Instead, I searched through my sleep befuddled brain and landed on something a mite more politic. "I'll think on it."

"You've got a lot of things to think about."

"Seems like."

"Maybe you could think on what you want to do for supper while you're at it."

I peered over my shoulder at him and the fading sunlight glimmering through the curtains. "We been asleep that long?"

"We were up all night." His hips pressed into mine and a wicked grin stretched his mouth. "Speaking of being up all night."

I laughed and rolled over, embracing him full on, and smiled.

Ever thing was gonna come up roses with me and Riley from now on. I didn't need no seeing from Old Mother to ken that.

EPILOGUE

A coupla weeks later, bright and early one Saturday morn, I slipped out from under Riley's watchful gaze and walked up to Henry's spot alongside the trail between my roost and Fame's. It was too cool out still, though the days lengthened a mite with each passing minute. A patch of blue wavered overhead, fighting for space above the fog clinging to the hills.

I shivered in my denim jacket and perched on the bench beside the tiny angel I placed there, soon as I scraped up the money for it after Henry passed. Daffodil shoots pressed up against the forest floor and a spate of crocuses bloomed, their purple heads tilting toward the angel like they was saying grace.

A faint breeze blowed across the space, tickling my nose, and I rubbed at it good with cold-stiffened fingers. "Henry, baby, is that you?"

The barest hint of a child's laughter drifted to me and faded away, and I was so thankful for the goodness of it, I coulda cried. Old Mother was wrong. My Henry hadn't turned evil, like she predicted.

But he would, if I didn't let him go.

Footsteps crunched up the trail behind me. I knowed without turning exactly who it was by the thread binding us together, the mother magic we conjured the night Missy put Brenyn down like the rabid dog she was and them young'uns crawled into freedom. Nora was a part of me now, same as Missy and Libby, but she was different. They was kinfolk. Their place in my life was earned by love and blood. Nora was a part of me because of sacrifice.

She give up an awful lot to help us out. I weren't never gonna forget how much.

Which is why when she was discharged from the hospital, I offered her Henry's room 'til we could find a safe place for her. It was time to clean out his room anyhow, time to give his toys and clothes to some kid what needed 'em. Lord knowed Henry didn't need 'em no more, and neither did I.

His passing still hurt, don't get me wrong, but the hurt had eased enough for me to realize that holding onto him did more harm than good. He'd always be a part of me. That weren't gonna change. But now I needed to make room for something else, something good and whole and right.

So the day after that big fight, I went through his things and picked out the stuff I couldn't bear to part with, and I shared it all with Riley. The paper where Henry writ out his name for the first time. The plaster cast of his handprint from some forgotten vacation Bible school at the church up the road. The Star Wars Lego set he put together, all by his own self.

Riley stood in the middle of the room holding that prize, staring at it for so long, I finally asked if he was ok.

"I wish I'd known him," he said, his voice gruff and tight.

I set down the box I was gonna empty Henry's chest of drawers into and placed a hand over Riley's heart. "You do know him, honey, right here, same as me."

He nodded and sniffed and turned away without saying a word, but I saw the tear slipping down his cheek. Right then and there, I vowed to do ever thing in my power to make sure my Riley never cried another tear again.

The bench sagged gently under Nora's weight, bringing me back to the present.

"It's a beautiful spot," she said.

I nodded. Yup, it was beautiful. We'd worked to make it so, to erase the blood my grandma spilled when she took my boy's life over something so stupid as him not having enough painter in him.

I'd always wondered why she hadn't been content letting him grow up among the Panther Clan, where the painter woulda rubbed off on him. I reckoned that, like me, it never woulda rubbed off enough for him to be a true two-natured the same as his cousins. It woulda drove him crazy or left him hanging between one and t'other, and if his contact with the Clan was cut off, he woulda died from the lack, same as in them stories I read. I had to be careful with Riley, but for me anyhow, hanging around them painters was worth the risk, just to know that side of my family, so long denied me by hatred.

Nora's hand slid gentle like over mine. "It's time, Sunny."

I nodded again and stood up, facing her now, and heaved out a huge breath. "I'm gonna miss the little rugrat."

"No, Sunny. You can't miss what's held in your heart."

She pulled a bundle of dried herbs out of a paper sack, being careful with her cast. Sage and a bunch of other stuff I couldn't identify by smell or looks. "I'm going to start by cleansing the area, then we'll work on helping Henry move to the next plane of existence."

I helped her light the herbs and douse the flames, and stood back as she wafted smoke to the four corners, murmuring her witchy spells while I stood on and watched. Truth be told, I was grateful for her help, grateful to have another friend. She misspoke that day in the hospital. Sure, I had her back, but the brunt of it was that she had mine. How many people would risk losing such a big part of their life to help a bunch of strangers out?

But Nora had. She done the right thing, just like that good heart of hers had told her to, and her heart was good. I could feel it, now that we was bound together somewhat.

And so, me and Missy and Libby and some others was searching for a place where Nora could lay low for a while, close enough for us to keep an eye on her if she needed us, not so close her old coven would come a-hunting for her. I was thinking Sylva was a nice spot. It was close to Qualla, the Eastern Band's main territory right there around Cherokee, and not so far from Asheville Nora couldn't get some city time in.

Bless her, but if ever there was a city folk born and bred, it was Nora.

Anyhow, word was already spreading from Cherokee to kin to friends to strangers up that way. A shop was about to come up for rent, one with a living space attached and a good yard for herbs and such, a place where Nora could start rebuilding her life, if she was of a mind to.

I reckoned she didn't have much choice, 'less she wanted to hightail it back to the safety of her own kin. For some reason, I was nigh on certain she was gonna stick around these parts for a while.

As for me, well. That was gonna take some doing. For the first time in so long I couldn't remember, I felt free, clean, empty. I fought my baby's monsters and my own and laid 'em all to rest. Maybe they was more monsters for me to fight, waiting just down the road and outta sight, but that was a bridge I'd cross when I come to it.

For now, I was content holding onto the good what come to me when I weren't looking, and that's about all a body could do in the short span allotted to us here on Earth.

ABOUT

Celia Roman lives in the Southern Appalachians, surrounded by generations of family and myth. Her stories are inspired by a natural interest in the paranormal and too many late night reruns of *Supernatural*. Find her online at:

www.celiaroman.com

SUNSHINE WALKINGSTICK SERIES
Hunter
Greenwood Cove
The Deep Wood
Cemetery Hill
Witch Hollow
Devil's Branch
Vampire Alley

KAYA FOX SERIES
A Vision in Death

VANESSA KINLEY, WITCH PI SERIES
The Single Witch's Guide to Online Dating
Between a Witch and a Hard Place
A Witch and Her Familiar
Black Witch Rising
A Witch Called Justice

Printed in Great Britain
by Amazon

56489001R00129